I0653337

TAKE IT OFF

TAKE IT OFF

MARK TRYON

CUTTING EDGE

Copyright © 1953 Mark Tryon

The characters and events portrayed in this book are fictitious. Any similarity to
real persons, living or dead, is coincidental and not intended by the author.
No part of this book may be reproduced, or stored in a retrieval system, or
transmitted in any form or by any means, electronic, mechanical, photocopying,
recording, or otherwise, without express written permission of the publisher.

Take It Off was the title of the original, hardcover edition. The
subsequent paperback edition was titled *Of G-Strings & Strippers*

ISBN-13: 978-1-954840-31-7

Published by
Cutting Edge Books
PO Box 8212
Calabasas, CA 91372
www.cuttingedgebooks.com

Will they ever come to us, ever again,
The long, long dances,
On through the dark till the dim stars wane?
EURIPIDES, The Bacchae

CHAPTER ONE

The spotlight shot its surprise-pink beam through the smoke-filled fetid air over the heads of sweating men trembling with anticipation, to form a sharply defined circle on the purple velour act-curtain. A stir went through the house. Men shifted in their seats, restlessly, tensely. They stole glances at each other out of the corners of burning, embarrassed, eager eyes. They rubbed their moist palms together and settled themselves forward in their seats. A great gasp, like the sigh of a mastodon went through the theatre.

Then the voice came over the p.a. system—the oily, ingratiating voice that seemed to slide over lascivious tonsils.

"And now, ladies and gentlemen, the Brunswick Theatre takes great pleasure in presenting the star of our show, that luscious, passionate firebrand from Latin America—" the voice rose in a triumphant crescendo—"Margot Diego, that fizzling, sizzling tornado, fresh from the flaming nightclubs of Mexico City!"

The shirtsleeved band in the pit, which had whined and wheezed its way through an evening of tunes, all sounding alike, slammed into a brassy imitation of a Latin American conga. It too managed to sound like all the other melodies of the night.

But now Margot was there. She had slipped through the curtain and was posing sexily in the center of the circle of light.

Margot had the blackest hair and the whitest skin in burlesque. She was dressed in a flaming yellow gown which dragged on the floor and covered her completely. Draped over her shoulders was an imitation mink stole that reached to her knees and swayed with her every movement. Her long raven hair was piled on top of her head, forming a crown for the exotic Latin features that smiled invitingly at the sweating customers.

Her pose lasted only a second, then she moved forward, the circle of light following her as she swung to the left and strutted slowly toward the proscenium wall. Although she was fully clothed and abundantly covered, each movement managed to convey a sexual promise that tensed every man in the audience. She smiled languidly under long lashes, and tilting her head provocatively, made a small, obscene gesture with her hand, reaching out toward the men and bringing the half-closed fist slowly back toward her pelvis.

At the proscenium she turned and came back across the stage, her high heels sounding hollowly on the stage floor, her knees a little stiff, forcing her hips into an exaggerated sway.

Margot was the hit of the season. Men swarmed from Manhattan, from Long Island, from everywhere to see her—men who went boldly and men who went ashamedly. Men who told their wives who waited breathlessly for them to return so that the moment might be relived and fulfilled with the stimulus they had received. And men who lied to their wives because they could not tell them the truth. She was the promise and the fulfillment, the threat and the eternal whore. She was great.

Now, as she strutted from left toward right on the stage, swaying her hips, her mouth moving languorously as she muttered the words of the tune to herself, a man stepped into the lower right-hand box of the auditorium. His movement was slight and imperceptible—a bare parting of the curtains and a swift flutter as he slid inside to stand at the very rear of the box, his back against the curtain. He was dressed in an immaculate dinner jacket. He was obviously a gentleman, a man of about forty years of age, his slightly greying hair combed tightly to the top of a head whose features were sharp and aquiline. His right hand was in his jacket pocket. After he had entered the box he did not move, but stood like a statue, his features frozen and set.

As Margot reached the right proscenium wall, her hands described a swift arc to both sides, carrying the stole up and away from her gleaming shoulders. It seemed to swing through the air and then disappear out into the wings.

The audience heard her delighted laugh as she leaned briefly against the wall, her hands smoothing her hips which undulated slightly. Then she was away from the wall and moving left again.

Her hands went hesitantly toward the zipper between her breasts. She moved it down an inch and then removed her hands from it again. She looked questioningly out into the auditorium to await with obvious satisfaction the whispering, hissing, breathless, "Ye-e-e-s! Now! NOW! *Take it off!*" which always accompanied this teasing little trick. She smiled and swung rhythmically straight across the stage before her hands came back again, this time to rip the zipper straight down to the center of her lap. There was a gasp from the house, but she turned her back on the audience and undulated across the stage again, hearing the restless stirring behind her.

Reaching stage right, she turned two or three times in quick succession. Then she suddenly stepped out of the voluminous, all-covering yellow gown and threw it into the wings. She turned and faced the crowd.

Under the outer gown, she had been wearing a tight strapless burnt sienna brassiere that just managed to confine her full, swaying breasts. From the bra she was naked, down across white, taut ribs and slightly rounded abdomen with its deep, shadowy navel. Draped about her hips were the burnt sienna strippers' panels that swayed loosely, allowing generous glimpses of long white perfectly molded legs, full and heavy in the thighs.

3

She turned slowly around, revealing the fact that the panels were fastened around her so low that the very top of her curved lower torso was showing, flanked on either side by a deep, lascivious dimple.

Then she laughed again and disappeared off into the wings. Only the circle of light remained behind, waiting, hovering, promising ...

The audience roared, stamped its feet, slammed its palms together, whistled and screamed.

Margot, standing just off in the wings, pulled her brassiere tighter and tugged the panels down until they were perched so precariously on her hips that it seemed that only a miracle was holding them up.

Now the rhythm of the band changed as it brassed its way into a swift, torrid rumba. Margot braced one foot behind her and catapulted onto the stage. The men in the audience roared their delight. She flung herself forward until she hit center of the stage. Here she stopped, laughed out loud, and flung her hips into a series of bumps and grinds so violent that they could almost hear her body swinging and twirling. She parted her knees and squatted to the floor, her hips working. She leaned back on her hands, her pelvis aimed straight down into the house.

Men leaned forward, twisted toward the side to try to catch a glimpse of forbidden pleasures. But Margot's panels clung tightly down between her legs, only stirring and bumping slightly with her violent movement.

Then she was on her feet again, writhing, her hands now reaching avidly out toward the men, pulling and straining and tugging them toward her flailing hips. Her eyes were rolling in their sockets, giving the impression that if she could have hurled herself into the laps of this multitude of hungry men, she would have rolled and screamed with mad, abandoned laughter and given herself until she had been killed in the orgy.

The audience felt it and rose to the occasion. The quiet man in the box felt it, too, and his mouth drew into a taut, white line of distaste. He dropped his eyes with shame, seemingly unable to look at this display of sexuality. His fingers tightened on the object in his pocket.

Suddenly Margot was on her feet, her breath coming in swift choking gasps. Slowing down her movements, she moved toward the left of the stage. Here she turned her back toward the audience, bent over and rolled her buttocks in long, slow rolls. Straightening up, her hands moved behind her back to unfasten the brassiere. She turned around, holding it against her chest with both hands, and smiling slightly through parted lips, she walked quietly to the right again.

Nonchalantly she threw the brassiere into the wings after the rest of her clothes and stood again facing the men in the house. She was wearing a thin net strippers' bra through which her breasts showed clearly.

And now, to those who had not seen Margot before, it became abundantly clear why she was as successful as she was in her business. Although she was of only medium height, her breasts were very large. But they were taut and full—rare in a woman as small as she was.

She ran her hands gently and clingingly over the swaying fullness and down over her hips. Then she bumped her way across the stage again, her breasts swinging free and unhampered above her rolling hips.

When she reached left stage, she surprised everyone by suddenly jerking off her panels and disappearing into the wings, leaving behind her a fleeting memory of white nakedness.

The audience went mad and on the hurricane of sound, she returned to the stage, practically nude. Margot did not believe in decorated G-strings. She adhered to the school of simulated nakedness as being the most effective stock in a stripper's trade. Now, as she appeared the men in the audience saw a snowy white, roundly curved body, covered only by a net brassiere and a tiny white satin G-string. The spotlight faded from the comparative brightness of the surprise-pink to the gently clothing quality of red.

Her body seemed to flame, and as the tempo of the orchestra was stepped up, she hurled herself into a frenzy of writhing. She tore down her black hair until it was cascading about her heaving shoulders. She rubbed herself madly against the curtains; she squatted with her knees wide, almost upon the floor.

Then, in a dead silence which seemed to breathe with anticipation, with tenseness and with the strain of unfulfilled desire, she rose slowly and with deliberate movements removed the confining net from her bosom. She flung her arms wide and stood there naked, her breasts heaving with the effort, her eyes glowing with triumph.

The shot rang out from the box, the stab of flame piercing the comparative darkness and Margot dropped to the floor without a sound. From a small hole below her left breast, blood commenced trickling slowly down over her body, across her flesh to disappear in the deepening valleys of her groin.

The theatre was as still as a tomb.

Lula Lang waited in the wing, standing there during Margot's act, watching with fascinated loathing, unable to take her eyes off the white, gyrating body.

A small, golden blonde, she was the very opposite of Margot. Over her rested an aura of innocence. Her soft hair hung loosely and gently about her shoulders. She was dressed in a long white gown, reminiscent of a bride, and over her head, hiding her small clean features and little cherry mouth, hung a thin veil which strengthened the impression of virginity and the mystery of an unknown woman, untouched and chaste.

The shot jerked her violently out of her reverie. It slashed and stabbed into her pattern of life like a knife suddenly ripped through the canvas of an already satisfactorily completed painting. It was a blinding flash of lightning, illuminating a comfortably dusky corner in which life sat crouched, having already made its compromise and decided to stay put, hiding in the safety of darkness, huddling in the womb of night.

Lula's eyes dilated and she staggered back, her hands clutching frantically at the velour of the wing-leg.

Then, while Margot's exotic life slowly trickled out into the inexorable sea of infinity, while the sudden silence in the theatre exploded into a madhouse of screaming, wailing sound, while two iron fists clamped down on the shoulders of the man in the dinner jacket, while the bewildered orchestra wheezed and coughed over its brasses for a short while until the conductor, with a presence of mind which he was to describe with unlimited pride for the rest of his days, drove them into a frenzy of noisy orchestration, and while the curtain dropped abruptly to allow for the removal of the bleeding nakedness on the stage, Lula slid slowly along the drape and onto the floor, to lie there, a crumpled heap, her face hidden in her arms.

A young man, dressed in baggy-pants comedian's costume, came running around the drape and dropped to his knees next to the fallen girl.

"Lula!" he cried, "Lula, don't! Look up at me, Lula!" He pushed his arms under her inert form and tried to pull her to a sitting position.

"Look, Lula," he pleaded, "It is all over. Come with me, honey, let's get out of this sinkhole and never come back!"

"It's too late now."

"It's not too late! Please, Lula, let me take you out of this. We could do so many wonderful things together!"

But she pushed him away violently, and as he fell back she cried, "Leave me alone, Luke! Go away! I don't ever want to have anything to do with you! Oh, God! Oh, God!" Sobbing uncontrollably, she slumped again to the floor. The drapes, the floor, the theatre, the building, the city whirled and spun and careened like a whirlpool.

At the center was Lula Lang, the "Blonde Sensation," "Everyman's Bride," "The Essence of Innocence." The sensation of the day and the dream of all masculinity!

CHAPTER TWO

The dream was the answer of the Brunswick Theatre to the hunger of mankind. Night after night, and afternoon after afternoon, the dusty, musty old stage echoed with the lasciviousness, with the latent bawdiness of the American male. It was in the business of giving him free vent for his emotions. It fulfilled this destiny with its strippers, with its lavish chorus interludes and with its frank, direct comedians.

(STREET SCENE)

(*Luke, all spiffed up in a zoot-suit—baggy, peg-bottom pants, a long jacket, tight at the waist, a wide-brimmed hat, and a chain that drags behind him on the floor, walks on stage with the sexy Redhead, barely covered by a tight-fitting green dress.*)

REDHEAD: That was a wonderful date, honey.

LUKE: OK, OK, let's go upstairs then, and you can show me how much you enjoyed it.

REDHEAD: Aw, honey, you know I can't do that.

LUKE: What's the matter? What's the matter? Are you …?

REDHEAD: Aw, no, it's nothing like that. My grandmother is asleep in the next room.

LUKE: Well, we'll give her some, too! I got enough for everybody. (*Lascivious leer at audience, which snickers.*)

REDHEAD: Aw, no, grandma is ninety years old! Besides she's got a wooden leg.

LUKE: We'll be quiet.

(*Grandpa walks on. It is "Little Jack" Horner, glasses just barely hanging on at the end of his nose. He is wearing a long, dragging flannel robe with a fantastic design on it. His white wig sticks out in every direction.*)

GRANDPA: What's going on here?

REDHEAD: Oh, grandpa, this is Luke Lucas. We just had a date.

GRANDPA: (*Raising cane*) Get out of here you mugwump! You came here last week. I heard you, making all that noise in the next room! Get out of here!

REDHEAD: You see what I said?

GRANDPA: Let me catch you back here one more time and I'll beat your brains out! (*He turns and stalks out.*)

REDHEAD: Now, go away, will you, Luke? You embarrass me in my own home!

LUKE: Please, honey! Can't we work something out?

REDHEAD: Oh, all right. Wait half an hour, then come quietly up the back stairs. My room is the first one on the right. Now remember, it is the first one on the right, *not* on the left. That is grandma's room.

LUKE: (*Panting*) The first one on the right, *not* on the left. That is grandma's room.

REDHEAD: That's right. You come up real quiet and be quiet while you are there.

LUKE: (*Panting*) All right! All right, honey!

(*Redhead leaves stage.*)

LUKE: (*Turning to audience*) Oh, brother, did you get a gander at that? Am I going to have me a time! (*He leaves the stage.*)

GRANDPA: (*Rushing on stage*) Susie! Susie!

(*Redhead enters.*)

REDHEAD: What is it, Grandpa?

GRANDPA: Oh gee! Oh golly! Your grandma is dead! We'll have to bury her in the morning.

(*Redhead weeps violently and she and grandpa leave stage. Dimout to fade up again almost immediately.*)

LUKE: (*Enters, rubbing his hands together*) Boy, did I have a time last night. Boy, oh boy! Was that good!

REDHEAD: (*Enters*) Good morning, Luke!

LUKE: (*Slobbering*) Good morning, you wonderful thing! Oh gosh, are you wonderful! (*He tries to embrace her*) I love you, I love you, I love you! (*He leers at the audience.*)

REDHEAD: What are you talking about, you no-good bum! What happened to you last night?

LUKE: What do you mean, what happened to me last night?

REDHEAD: Why didn't you come?

LUKE: Why didn't I come? What do you mean, I didn't come? (*He leers at audience.*)

REDHEAD: I waited for you half the night.

LUKE: What are you talking about? I had a wonderful time with you.

REDHEAD: With me?

LUKE: Why, certainly. I came up the stairs quiet as a mouse and into the apartment from the back. I took the first door to the left ...

REDHEAD: (*Wailing*) Left?

LUKE: Sure! That's what you said!

REDHEAD: I said right! *Right!* You went in grandma's room, and she is *dead!*

LUKE: (*Hitting himself over the head*) Damn! And I gave her five bucks, too!

(BLACKOUT)

This was Lula's life.

She stood in the wings watching Luke and Susie and Little Jack Horner unraveling their instinctive timing. She listened to the roars of the men in the audience and she marveled at the faces lit by the general lighting on the stage. The blank doll-face of Susie the straight-woman, the subtly evil face of "Little Jack" who specialized in bumpkin comedy and the youthful, laughing face of Luke Lucas, twenty-three, ambitious, always quoting the eventual possibilities of a comic who had started in burlesque, giving the names of all the great stars who had commenced on the slanting boards of slapstick.

And she wondered how she had ever gotten into this …

It was very simple, really. Too simple and too commonplace to be picturesque. It happened every day. The ancient story of the small town girl come to the big city to make good. Two years in a good college drama department, playing ingenues and an occasional character part. The polite, educated audience applauding her until she thought she was God's gift to the theatre.

Polite dates with fraternity boys a little overawed by her prominence as the beautiful star of the campus, trying to make her because she was in *that* profession and consequently, being a passionate actress, probably "put out." Laughing up her sleeve at the frustrated boys, dreaming of the great day, passing her courses with honors because she was bright, working hard and thinking, when the diploma was shoved into her hand that the great, shiny door was wide open and all she had to do was walk in.

Coming to New York, her shiny, unscarred luggage in her hand, finding a room in the Village and going, expectantly, on her second day in the city to the first agent whose address she had, knowing full well that he would roll out the carpet and call big producers on the phone about his marvelous find.

And on that fateful second day discovering that she was nobody! But nobody! The agent smiling indulgently. Promising to call her "if anything turns up."

And then the walks! The interminable, endless, exhausting walks from door to door, from politely smiling man to politely smiling man, from secretary to secretary, from front desk to front desk.

The ghoulish hope of "Television auditions," attended by four hundred young girls exactly like herself with the same eager, fresh young faces, one like the other. The "Readings" for agents and for possible future productions, attended by the same girls and three hundred clean-cut young men breathing ostentatiously about being "at liberty," hiding the fray on their pants with fresh creases created by the simple expedient of putting them under the mattress while they slept.

The wonderful bohemian parties in small rooms and apartments in the Village, talking brightly about "The Theatre" and "Art" and swilling lukewarm Chianti while the hopes were slipping and the ennui of frozen terror settled over them.

Finally her little money had given out. Her parents, who had put her through college at real sacrifice to themselves, had managed to beg, borrow, and scrape up enough for her to last two months in New York. That was all the time she would need. She was sure of that. Back home in Centerville, they hung breathlessly on every letter she wrote. They expected much of their daughter. The citizens expected much of the young, startling girl with her exotic ambitions who had left to put the town on the map. There had been so much talk of how the town could benefit from her being a famous star. Her parents had sunk so much money in the project. Much more than they could afford.

She could not disappoint them.

She went to Hansel Schnitzler, booking agent for the burlesque circuit.

She ran from his office in terror and confusion when she discovered something about the facts of life.

She returned to the Village and spent her last two dollars on a loaf of bread and a bottle of Chianti. She had a party and everyone cried and quoted effectively from Shakespeare and she decided to go back to Centerville and find a husband the next day.

But in the morning there was the letter from her folks. It reiterated the very hopes of Centerville, the dreams of her parents. Their pride and high expectations.

And she could not go home.

She returned to Hansel Schnitzler.

The dark-haired girl at the desk looked up, her unbelievable breasts pointing straight at Lula across the typewriter. She spoke with a nasal twang.

"Yeah, honey?"

"I … I'd like to see Mr. Schnitzler."

The girl looked her up and down. "You was here yesterday, wasn't you?"

"Yes."

The girl smiled nastily. "Can't you take no for an answer?"

"He … he didn't say no."

"I know … you ran out on him. He didn't think much of it."

"I'm sorry. He … he just sort of startled me."

"He ain't got much use for kids that ain't dry behind the ears."

Lula was getting so nervous that she was growing angry. "Look, I just want to see *him*. Is he in?"

"What if he is?"

Lula shouted, "I want to see Mr. Schnitzler!"

The door to the inner sanctum opened and an elderly man was practically hurled through its maw. He had a small, innocent-looking pink face. There were tears in his eyes. He was followed immediately by a huge man with little wisps of greying hair around a deadwhite, bald dome. The moist stump of a cigar was stuck fiercely between his yellow teeth. His small eyes were narrowed, mean-looking. He gave the indistinct impression of getting some sort of evil pleasure out of what he was doing.

"Now listen to me, Anderson … for the last time! There ain't room for you in show business any more. Soft-shoeing and patter is dead! Do you hear me? It's dead! So will you quit cluttering up my office?"

The old man ran blindly out into the hall and Schnitzler slammed the door after him. Then he turned to the secretary, who was snickering ingratiatingly.

"Next time that little runt comes in here looking to bother me, tell him to get the hell out and stay out!"

He was starting back into his office when Lula, in desperation, stepped into his path and he was forced to notice her. He stopped briefly and glared at her, his cigar rolling obscenely in his discolored mouth. Then he turned to the secretary again. "And that goes for this chicken, too," he said and started out again.

But Lula was in his way. "Please, Mr. Schnitzler," she said, "I'd like to talk to you."

"Look, kid, I don't mess with chickens like you. 'Show me your legs,' I says, and you tear out of here like I'd tried to make you. Well, look, you ain't so makeable, so don't flatter yourself."

"I'm sorry, Mr. Schnitzler. It was just that it was the first time I'd had to do something like that."

"I know, I know. I get dozens of them. Little mama's girls with college educations and the hots for neon lights. Well, look, I deal with *women*. Real, grownup women, who ain't scared of nothing. So take your little corpse out of here and back to mama and don't bother me again."

"I'm not scared of anything any more, Mr. Schnitzler."

"No? What's the matter? You hungry? You in trouble? *Can't* go home to mama?"

"I just want a job."

"All right. We'll see how bad you want one. Come on in the office."

He preceded her through the door and Lula followed meekly, the secretary leering at her before she returned to her frenzied typing.

Mr. Schnitzler threw himself on a long, low couch which stood against one wall. He waved her toward a chair by the desk, but Lula was too nervous to sit down. She stood before him, her legs pressed closely together.

"Relax, girlie," he drawled. "Sit down and rest your rear."

She shook her head determinedly.

"OK, stand then. I don't give a hang. Now if you ain't too scared, tell me what you're after."

"I ... I'm looking for a job."

"Yeah, I know. They all are. What kind of a job?"

"Anything ..." And before she knew it, standing there like a lost child before him she blurted out the whole sorry tale of her stardom in college, her high hopes and her consequent disappointments.

"Look, girlie, *girlie!*"

She stopped talking in confusion and stood waiting.

"I've heard all this before. Now, be realistic. What can you *do?*"

"I can act."

"Oh, nuts! Who says so? A bunch of college professors?"

"Everybody who has ever seen me has said so."

"Has Atkinson said so? Has Kazan said so? Has Metro-Goldwyn-Mayer said so? How the hell do you know you can act, college girl?"

Lula's eyes started to fill with tears.

"Look, girlie. I've seen hundreds of you. Maybe thousands. 'I can act! They all told me so in college!' So what? The woods are full of you. I ain't asking if you can act. Any kid can act a little. What can you *do?* Have you got a specialty? Can you sing? Can you dance? Can you do bumps and grinds? What the hell can you *do?*"

Lula stared at him in bewilderment.

"See? That's what I thought. You know all about theatre history and the plays of that screwball Frenchman, what's his name? Satyr? But you can't *do* nothing!"

"I can sing a little."

"A little? So what. So can I. Would you care to pay six bucks a seat to hear me sing? No? I thought not. Neither would anybody else. Anybody can sing a little, just like anybody can act a little. The customers pay for specialties."

"I can learn."

"All right! Now you're talking! Now relax and answer my questions. Sit down, I can't talk to a woman standing up like a schoolkid. Sit down!"

Lula sat limply on the chair by the desk, her knees close together.

"Look at you," sneered Hansel. "Demure, ain't you? A cute little chicken with your knees close together. Off-pink suit, sweet little hat, discreet make-up. Butter wouldn't melt in your mouth! Have you ever been in bed with a man?"

"N … no."

"No, I thought not! Too good for it, ain't you? What the hell do you know about life? Get a job singing in church. What do you come to me for?"

"Please, Mr. Schnitzler. That was not what I came here for."

"You don't know what you came here for," he snapped. "You don't know nothing about it. Do you know that I don't book nothing but burlesque?"

"Yes, sir."

" 'Yes, sir,' " he sneered, "do you know anything about burlesque? Have you ever stripped down before a bunch of starving, snarling, leering men? No, of course you haven't. You'd be scared of it, wouldn't you? Those naughty, naughty men, giving in to such a nasty urge. Oh, great," he groaned, "I know you. I've seen hundreds of you."

Angrily, Lula leaped to her feet and started out of the office. Hansel laughed and as he laughed he shook and as he shook the room trembled.

"Are you mad now? Good! Now, if you're mad enough, maybe we can talk business. How bad do you want a job?"

Lula stopped by the door. "It's none of your business! I'm not going to sit here and listen to any more of your insults! The … the *hell* with you!" She turned again, ready to stalk out of the door.

With amazing agility he was up and by her side, a hand firmly on her arm. "All right, all right, honey, that's enough. Now come back here and talk to Uncle Hansel." He pulled her gently back until she stood before the couch again, then he returned to his former position, legs a-spraddle before him.

"Now, look, honey. The only way a man can find out if there's any spunk in a woman like you is to get her mad. If you'd just started bawling and run out of this office again as you did yesterday I'd have let you go, and good riddance to you, but if you can get mad enough to cuss me out, then there's hope for you. So listen to me closely now."

Lula stood still and waited, still seething, but with hope growing within her.

"As I said, all I book is burlesque. Consequently, all I'm looking for is funny comedians and good-looking women, who ain't afraid of taking it off, and who have enough spunk in them to get the customers excited. Now, there ain't nothing wrong with your looks. Nice little figger. Cute little face. Good blonde hair. You wouldn't look bad in a chorus, or even with a specialty. Now, are you willing to exploit that, to learn what little bit of 'dancing' will be expected of you to keep a job, hopping around with the other gals?"

Lula smiled a little. "Yes, Mr. Schnitzler, I am."

"Good! All right, now we're getting somewhere. Do you realize that you're getting into the oldest and the dirtiest profession in the world? The theatres ain't equipped with perfumed dressing-rooms. They stink of sweat and cheap perfume and mildewed costumes. You'll be doin' four-a-day, not just an evening show with an occasional matinee, and in the morning you'll be staggering through rehearsals for the next show. You'll be spending half your time pulling knives out of your back and you'll have to fight off the stage-door-Johnnies if you want to retain your precious virginity. Nobody is going to notice you, or even pay any attention to you. You'll be a nobody, a cute figger and a nice pair of gams in the second line. If you're lucky you might get a chance, eventually, to strip naked in front of a houseful of raving men."

"Mr. Schnitzler. This is just a stopgap."

"Oh, I've heard that one before, too. Well, never mind. Do you realize what you're getting into?"

"Yes, sir."

"Well, all right, then!" Hansel's eyes lit up almost imperceptibly. "Let's see what you've got."

"What I've got?"

"Yeah, yeah, your legs and whatever else you might have in your favor. Hoist your skirts."

Lula turned beet-red, but obediently she lifted her skirts to just above her knees. The sheer stockings displayed lovely slim columns that rounded softly at the lower thigh.

Hansel groaned. "Girlie," he said with an elaborate show of patience, "burlesque don't quit at the knees! All the way up."

"*All* the way?"

"Yeah, all the way. Clear up to the panties. Clear up to the waist.

Lula hesitated for a long moment.

Hansel started to stand up. "All right, never mind, precious. If you've got something hidden up there that is a secret and that I ain't never seen before, you'd better keep it until the right man comes along."

Lula made a quick and desperate movement. "No, no, wait. I'll do it."

"Fine," he drawled, "what a break for Uncle Hansel. "All right, let's see it. All of it."

Lula, blushing furiously and trembling like a leaf, slowly pulled her skirt clear up around her waist and stood revealed before the fat man in her sheer little panties and brief garter-belt.

Hansel took a deep breath and stared unashamedly at the revelation.

The slim legs were long and beautifully turned columns of soft whiteness that looked satin-soft above the tops of the stockings. The tender thighs rose to the slanting, bottom edges of thin, white panties that were completely transparent.

Lula was well aware of this and was startled to find that aside from a burning sense of outraged modesty, she was shaking a little with a vague and pleasurable thrill at being thus revealed.

Hansel spoke hoarsely. "Keep it up and turn around."

Lula turned as slowly as the jerking of her knees would allow her.

Schnitzler stared at the small, rounded curves that shone like white globes through the sheer material. Then he sighed deeply. "Drop it," he said. Then after a pause, he added, "Not bad. Not bad. All right, let's see the rest of it."

Lula looked at him wide-eyed. "The rest?"

"Yeah, the chest, the bosoms, whatever you call them. Let's see them."

"Is … is that necessary?"

"What the hell do you think you're going to be selling to the customers? Shakespeare? Come on, or forget it. I can't represent something I haven't ever seen. If I'm going to handle this merchandise, I got to know what quality it is."

Slowly, she unbuttoned her suit-jacket. She took it off with trembling fingers, pulled her slip straps down and tucked her arms through them until they were hanging around her waist. Then she reached back, unsnapped her white satin brassiere and took it off. She stood before him, quietly and breathlessly.

Her breasts were small and white and round. They were like the breasts of a fifteen year old girl, not yet fully formed, but formed enough to startle the beholder with their promising softness and roundness. They rounded softly out from her chest with no sharp crease below them.

Hansel took a deep breath. "Yeah," he whispered, "yeah, I guess I can sell this merchandise, all right."

Lula, a deep feeling of shamed triumph coursing violently through her veins, put her clothes back on. When she was dressed, she sank limply into the chair, her eyes averted, her knees still trembling with the tension of the experience.

For a long time no one said anything.

Finally Schnitzler spoke. His voice was a little hoarse with the strain. "I'll place you, girlie, don't you worry. When do you want to go to work?"

"Anytime," Lula almost whispered, "tomorrow if it is possible."

"I'll see what I can do." His casualness seemed forced, unreal, as he waved his imperious hand toward the door, and Lula got up and started blindly out of the room, her cheeks still scarlet, her knees still trembling.

As she reached the door, it was swung open and a dark, medium-height woman with the almond-shaped eyes of a Latin came rushing into the room. She was dressed in a smart afternoon frock and a short mink cape. She wore no hat over her blue-black hair which was coiled on top of her delicate head.

The two women collided violently. The breath was almost knocked out of both of them and for a brief second they stood glued together in the doorway. Then, as they parted, Lula got a lightning glimpse of two deep dark eyes into which she seemed to sink and which looked at her with glowing interest. And as they drew apart, she felt herself gently pushed by the other woman's hands, the talon-like fingers digging intimately into the soft flesh of her breast and thigh. It appeared to be an accident, but somehow Lula knew it wasn't and as she hurried past the woman and through the outer office, she felt the hot eyes drilling holes in her back and fastening themselves on her agitated hips. She stumbled out and into the elevator, terribly conscious of her thumping heart.

She was clear out on the street before she realized that she had not left her name and address with Hansel Schnitzler's secretary.

After Lula had stumbled through the outer office and had disappeared out into the hall, Margot Diego turned to the agent, still sitting on the couch.

"Who was that girl, Hansel?" she asked in a soft, purring voice.

Only then did Schnitzler stir. He sat up straight and gave vent to a long, heartfelt curse. "Dammit, she didn't even tell me her name and address!"

He leaped to his feet and ran through the outer office into the hall. But Lula had disappeared. When he returned, he looked very dejected. "Well," he muttered, "maybe I didn't scare her away completely. Maybe she'll be back." He went into his own room where Margot was waiting.

"Who *was* she?" Margot asked again.

"I don't know. She never told me, she was that scared. But she sure as hell was a beauty.'

Margot sat on the edge of the desk, sheer silk stockings showing above perfectly rounded knees. "Are you thinking of adding her to your ... collection?" she asked quietly. There was just the barest suggestion of a threat in her voice.

Hansel growled, "It's none of your business."

"Isn't it, Hansel? Every girl you add to your collection is a threat to me, isn't she? How do I know you're not getting tired of me?"

"Margot, who said anything about getting tired of you?"

"Oh, you wouldn't say anything, Hansel, not you. It's what would happen to my bookings that would show your true feelings."

"Well, nothing is going to happen to your bookings."

"Nothing had better."

Hansel started to get mad. "Now look here …"

"Don't get mad, Hansel, it looks like hell when you begin to quiver like that. You're not exactly what I'd call beautiful under normal circumstances, but when you get mad, you get positively ludicrous."

Schnitzler turned his back and went over and threw himself on the couch in his favorite position, legs a-spraddle to accommodate his tremendous stomach. "All right," he sighed, "what do you want this time? More money? A different booking? Or what?"

Margot smiled languidly and slipped the fur jacket off her shoulders. Her full breasts stood out in bold relief. "I had something on mind when I came up here, but I guess the sight of that girl chased it straight out of my mind."

Hansel sat up straight, his face registering considerable alarm, his hands fluttering ineffectually in the air. "Now, you leave that girl alone, Margot!"

"Why? Do you have her picked out all for yourself?"

"I don't want you fooling with her."

"I want you to put her in my show. Find a spot for her."

"I won't do it. She's a good kid. I don't want her to get anywhere near you."

"What's the matter with *me*, Hansel? What are you so squeamish about?"

"You know what I'm talking about. I'm not going to supply *you* with girls."

"You don't have to supply me with *girls*, Hansel. I just want that one."

"I won't do it."

"I'm afraid you'll have to, Hansel."

"I don't even know her name and address."

"You'll find her, I'm sure. And when you do I want her in my show."

Hansel cursed wildly and finally almost screamed, "No! No! You can't have her!"

Margot stood up, a small smile of triumph hovering about her scarlet mouth. She made an elaborate ceremony of putting on her mink jacket as she spoke. "If that girl is not in my show within four days, Hansel, I am going to feel that it is my duty as a wife to inform Frank of the little sessions you have made me have with you ever since I first came to you for a job. What do you think he will have to say when he hears about our little private stripping parties and about your fat hands feeling me up? Think about that, you eunuch!"

And she went quietly out of the office, leaving a badly frightened, trembling fat man sitting on the couch.

Hansel muttered curses between his teeth ...

CHAPTER THREE

From the first afternoon in the business, Lula had been confronted with the special, tangy taste of American burlesque. Much of it she had not understood, but much of it she instinctively assimilated through her veins, because the bawdiness of burlesque is the bawdiness that goes back to Dionysus, to the lascivious rites in honor of the God of Fertility and the God of the Wine.

The show that she heard over the monitor system from the dressing room of the chorus was somehow not surprising to her. For Lula was a woman. A full-fledged woman ...

(*Little Jack on the p.a. system, doing a slushy rendition of "There's No Place Like Home" in his high, nasal tenor. Lights up "In-One" on a bedroom with a big iron double bed. A hatrack is at stage right. The back-drop is a wall with windows looking out over the city. The luscious Redhead is pacing the floor in a stunningly tight afternoon gown. She has a fur jacket draped over her shoulders and is wearing a chic little hat.*)

REDHEAD: Here it is half an hour since Joe said he'd come and pick me up. My husband is away and won't be back until tomorrow and Joe and I are going to have a little fun. Oh, damn! Why doesn't he come?

(*Enter, from right stage, Luke. Before you can say "Boo," he has flung his hat on the hatrack and has leaped out of his trousers and hung them beside the hat, by the suspenders. He is wearing red flannels and a long shirt that reaches almost to the floor.)*

LUKE: Hello, honey, here I am home a whole day early! Gosh, did I miss you! (*He runs to the bed and beats on it with his fist.*) Come on! Let's fly!

REDHEAD: Good heavens, my husband! What'll I tell him? (*Luke notices that the Redhead is all dressed up.*)

LUKE: What's this? What're you all dressed up for?

REDHEAD: I … I … I was on my way to visit mother …

LUKE: Your mother? She's been dead ten years!

REDHEAD: No … I … I mean … father …

LUKE: Where? In Alcatraz? (*He turns to audience.*) I smell a rat! (*Turns back to Redhead.*) You liar! Oh, you unfaithful slut, you! You weren't going to see nobody, you were getting ready to two-time me! (*He weeps elaborately as he sinks on the bed.*) Here I am, slaving so hard the blood is coming out from under my fingernails and except for five or six elderly ladies I have to see for business purposes, I have never been unfaithful to you. And you can do this to me! You can bring yourself to do this to me! (*He leaps up and rushes to hatrack.*) No! This is more than I can stand! I am leaving you! (*He rushes into his clothes with tremendous speed.*) Goodbye! (*He starts out right, but the Redhead flings herself after him and clutches his sleeve.*)

REDHEAD: No! No, Luke, don't leave me! *Please* don't leave me! (*She bawls realistically.*) What would I ever do without you?

LUKE: That's better. (*He returns to hatrack and whips out of his clothes again. He rushes to the bed and beats on it with his fist.*) Come on, baby, let's fly.

(*Redhead wrings her hands. She turns to the audience.*)

REDHEAD: I must warn Joe not to come up here now. (*She turns to Luke.*) Wait a little while, honey. There's something I must do first. I'll be right back. (*She starts out right.*)

LUKE: What? (*He screams with rage and tears his hair.*) Over my dead body! I know you! You're going to warn your lover, that that ... that ... *cad!* I'm leaving you!

(*He rushes to the hatrack again and tears into his clothes, first getting his pants on backwards. Then he starts out right. The Redhead reaches out to stop him and by accident gets a hold of the waist of his pants. The suspenders come loose and he plays the remainder of the scene, frantically hanging on to his trousers.*)

REDHEAD: No! No! Wait! I won't go! I'll stay here with you, sweetheart! Don't leave me!

(*Luke is struggling with his pants.*)

LUKE: That's better. (*He goes to the bed, this time without removing his clothes.*) Come on, then. I haven't had anything since yesterday.

(*The Redhead draws herself up.*)

REDHEAD: Since yesterday? You were in Chicago yesterday!

(*Luke is confused.*)

LUKE: Eh ... eh ... that's not what I meant. I meant ... eh ... wasn't it yesterday? My gosh, how time does fly!

REDHEAD: You have deceived me! (*She starts out right.*) I'm leaving you ... you roué!

(*Luke stands gaping after her. Finally he bursts into action.*)

LUKE: All right! All right! Leave me if you want to!

REDHEAD: I will!

LUKE: But before you go, take off that hat! I paid for that hat and you ain't going to carry it out of here! (*Redhead takes off hat and hangs it on hatrack. Then she starts out again.*) And that jacket, too. Where do you think you got that? I paid for it! (*Redhead takes off jacket and hangs it by the hat. She starts out again.*) And that dress! You ain't going out of here with that dress on! (*Redhead unzips dress and steps out of it. She hangs it up, too. She is now dressed in the tiniest of panties and brassiere. She is virtually naked. She struts out right again.*) Wait a minute! (*Luke surveys her from head to foot.*) Are you going out of here like that?

REDHEAD: Yes!

LUKE: Are you going down on the street like that?

REDHEAD: Yes!

LUKE: Are you going by the corner post office where all those men are always standing around?

REDHEAD: (*Defiantly*) YES!

LUKE: (*Digging in his pocket and producing a letter*) Then mail this letter!

(BLACKOUT)

The voices and the roar from the audience came over the monitor system in the chorus dressing room. Lula knew that the next spot was an acrobatic dance specialty, and after that was a featured stripper. She had plenty of time.

She was writing a letter to her folks in Centerville and the job was not an easy one. She stared thoughtfully at the pen her parents had given her for a graduation present and listened absentmindedly to the buzz of conversation in the room.

There were eighteen girls in the chorus of the Brunswick Theatre. They were a motley crew. Their ages ranged from eighteen to thirty and they included virtually every form of femininity in existence. But they all had that "chorus girl look" about them. When they were on the street there was no mistaking them. A little too much lipstick, a little too high in the heels, clothes a little too swanky, and a little too much obvious gaiety.

Right now they were all stripped down for action in the process of changing from one number into another, and the room was filled with a milling, stirring mob in a state of comparative nakedness. Most of the girls were wearing only the tiny strippers' panties which went under their costumes. Hardly a single one had on a brassiere. And what was revealed was not necessarily luscious. Much of it showed wear and tear. A lot of the girls were touching up their make-up and the odor of heavy theatrical powder was almost nauseating. That, and the stench of sweat. The girls did not always have time in between shows to shower in the meager bathing facilities provided by the economically minded management of the Brunswick Theatre. After three or four performances in a day, the odor of sweating women tended to become somewhat overpowering.

Lula had only been a member of the troupe for two days and she had not yet gotten used to the fetid atmosphere. Nor had she gotten used to the shrill incessant chatter about absolutely nothing, which was a constant irritant to her ears. Nor had she gotten used to the blasé manner in which the call-boy opened the door, stuck his head in, and yelled his cue-warnings without the slightest regard for the modesty of the half-naked women in the room. She tried to keep covered as much as she could, but she was not always successful.

It wasn't only the call-boy that bothered her. She had lived in dormitories at college and had therefore been used to seeing other naked girls in the shower room and to being seen herself. But the dressing room at the Brunswick was different. Here she was not an individual with certain private rights which were respected. She was just female flesh, constantly looked over by the others and appraised for its possible future menace as a competitor. Every time she removed her clothes to put on her skimpy costumes, she felt the eyes of the other girls, enviously or maliciously or good-naturedly surveying her charms and calculating their possible monetary value. It made her think of herself as a sirloin steak in a butcher's glass counter. It made her intensely self-conscious and uncomfortable.

But a job was a job. She was grateful that she could write her parents at least a little of the truth. That she was employed in a theatre. She stretched the truth somewhat and informed them that she was now on her way as an "actress." She knew this would please them, for they had high hopes for her career, as did the little town of Centerville. The letter was not entirely according to Hoyle, but it looked good when she signed it and put the name on the outside of the envelope: *The Brunswick Theatre* under her own name.

Her conscience bothered her a little, but knowing that she was a comparative nonentity in the company, she did not fear detection. It would please her parents and after all, they would never know the difference. Her father was an invalid and her mother had to stay home to take care of him. There wasn't a chance in the world that they would ever come to faraway New York to see her "act" in her new job. All they would ever need to know was that after their serious expenditure of money, their daughter had finally gotten her foot in the door and was on her way.

To Lula, the Brunswick Theatre and its motley chorus, of which she was a member, was still only a stopgap, a doorway which was to lead to better things. She would continue to see the agents and sooner or later she would graduate from burlesque into greater things.

Luke had said so. That was what the Brunswick meant to him.

Now that the letter was finished, signed and sealed, she allowed herself to think with fondness of the young comedian she had met almost as soon as she had entered the theatre.

Luke Lucas, whose sights were set for television. He had taken one look at her as she had timidly come in through the stage door. He had seen how uncomfortable and out-of-place she felt and had joked her into feeling better with his wonderful natural wit. She had been pleasantly surprised, had confidently expected anyone working in burlesque to be vulgar and obnoxious. But Luke had been the very opposite. A gentleman. And kindly.

He had told her a little of his ambitions. He had joked about being a baggy-pants funnyman and had informed her with a great show of comic secretiveness that burlesque, in spite of its hoary age, could not possibly last, and that he, Luke Lucas, was at present building an atomic bomb-shelter to protect himself from the awesome explosion when the Brunswick would finally blow up. He was building the shelter under a C.B.S. Television studio so that when the holocaust was all over and the television people began digging themselves out, they would find *him* as the very answer to their problems of comedy.

He joked that undoubtedly *that* was the only way he could break into television. Then he had gotten serious and told her with great earnestness that the Brunswick was only a stopgap on his way to greater things before the cameras.

She had believed him. He was so nice. And after all, it was only a stopgap for her too. She told him as much and he had jokingly referred to them as "The Team" from then on.

She had found him young, ambitious, delightful. It was a new world she had entered into, a world that frightened the very wits out of her, but it was good to know that even in new worlds there were people like herself. It was reassuring ...

Lula dug through her pocketbook until she found a stamp. She put it on the envelope, and wrapping a white terry-cloth bathrobe about her small figure, she went out into the hall to take the letter to the doorman's desk where the mailman would pick it up.

The doorman was a snaggle-toothed, tobacco-stained old character, who reached out as Lula came near him and patted her body, kneading the soft flesh between his fingers. She pulled away from him.

"You'll never get anywhere that way, girlie," he muttered.

Lula was about to give him a sharp reply when a quiet voice behind her said, "Why should she want to get anywhere with you, you repulsive old crumb?"

She turned and Luke was standing there, still hanging on to the baggy pants he had worn in the post office skit.

Lula laughed and together the two young people wandered off in the cavernous wings, while the doorman looked after them with leering envy.

In the upstage right corner of the huge space, they came upon a wagon-stage on which was perched an huge glass tank, an oversized aquarium, full of clear water. In this, a rather athletic young lady who went by the name of Merma divested herself of various layers of clothing four times a day. Merma was a nice kid whose real name was Barbara Jones. She had started out to be an Olympic swimmer, but had ended up as "a stripping fish" as she wryly labeled herself.

Lula and Luke sat down on the edge of the platform which stirred slightly under them, as the well-oiled wheels slid a little to one side. The water in the tank swished gently and the lilting music that accompanied the acrobatic dance now being performed on stage rose for a moment, then dropped off to a sensuous murmur.

"Just like Jones Beach," said Luke and smiled at her, sitting there so primly with her knees close together and the terry-cloth robe pulled tightly around her legs.

She smiled back and for a little while they sat in silence.

It came to Lula that this life was not so bad at all. Stagestruck as she was and had been as far back as she could remember, this phony Jones Beach illusion, under the blue safety-light glowing dimly high up on the brick wall like gentle moonlight, seemed to her to be eminently satisfactory.

Looking into herself, she realized for the first time with any clarity at all that like all stage-folks she preferred illusion to reality, and preferably an illusion imaginatively created out of her own artistic ingenuity. The sweaty dressing room, the greedy little eyes of Hansel Schnitzler, the pawing of Margot and the doorman, the prying eyes of the other girls, all the things that had served in the last few days to frighten her and to make her feel vaguely unclean fell away, and only the illusion was left—of peace, of seclusion. It was like a symbol of her theatre-dream. A reminder that things could be beautiful and exciting and romantic.

She saw with a sudden pang that Luke had much to do with it. She glanced sideways at him sitting beside her, lost in his own reverie, his own dream, which was not unlike her own. Although he looked ludicrous in his clownish make-up and costume, his clean-cut features and crisp, curly hair could not be hidden by the grease-paint, nor could the lanky, clean sweep of his attractive body.

Hansel's sneering query went through her head. "Have you ever been in bed with a man?" She looked again at Luke and a pleasurable thrill went through her.

As they sat there together in silence, Luke reached out and took her hand. For a short instant she thought about pulling it back, but then she decided to let it rest. It was a part of the illusion and it seemed very right.

Lula had had few experiences with men.

As she had grown older, she had vaguely realized that it was not so much that she was afraid of them, as it was that she was a little afraid of herself. During her senior year in high school a rather startling thing had happened to her.

She had been invited to the Easter dance by one of the school's football stars. She was very proud of having been noticed by so prominent a young man and although the other girls warned her against having anything to do with him, she dressed in her finest and went.

He was the very essence of a gentleman at the dance itself and she enjoyed herself enormously, scoffing in her mind at the timid girls who had tried to warn her. She looked forward to putting them in their places the next day.

Then the dance was over and they stopped at the local all-night cafe for hamburgers and coffee, and after that the boy said, "I guess I'd better take you home."

They went reluctantly, hand in hand, to his car and he started the motor. Before he pulled away from the curb, however, he asked ... oh, so casually, "Have you ever seen Waterworks Hill in the moonlight? You can see the whole town."

She shook her head innocently, and he continued, "Let's run up for just a minute."

She saw no harm in that and nestling back into the cushioned seat she murmured, "All right." She was deliciously drowsy and tremendously attracted to the clean-cut young athlete.

He drove up above the city to the barren loneliness above the water reservoir. There they sat for a long time, dreamily watching the city, his arm loosely about her shoulders. Finally he turned to her and it seemed strange that his breathing was not normal. She wondered vaguely whether he was not feeling well, but then he whispered, "What would you do if I kissed you?"

Something like that had been stirring vaguely in her own mind, she realized then, and she smiled languidly. "Why don't you try it and find out?"

He leaned over her and placed his lips gently against hers, his arm tightening about her shoulders. She put a hand at the back of his neck and pulled herself a little closer toward him. The small movement had a violent effect on him. He ground his mouth against hers and little by little the tip of his tongue forced her lips apart until her mouth was wide open and she was drinking him in with every panting breath.

She clung to him avidly, her own tongue exploring the inner reaches of his mouth, gasping for breath, moaning deep in her throat.

He made a small, triumphant, joyous noise and pulled her brutally against him. His trembling fingers pushed the thin straps of her gown down and unsnapped her tiny brassiere and his hand cupped a small, soft breast. She felt her flesh come alive, to push, turgid and taut, into the palm of his molding, caressing hand.

Thus they clung together for a long time, their hands moving frantically, caressing each other's bodies. Not a word further was exchanged between them.

After a while she felt the pressure on her breast released and his hand laid gently on her calf. It moved up slowly and inexorably to her knee, pushing her dress before it. Then it was on her thigh, rising above the stocking-top, gently sliding over the soft satiny skin it found there.

Suddenly she found that her long dress was bunched around her waist and she was sitting before him half-naked. His hand moved swiftly over her and she suddenly pulled back. "No, no, don't!"

It was not prudery or fear for her reputation or any of the conventional reasons that brought her up sharply. It was the stabbing, overpowering pang in her very loins that frightened her.

He removed his hand slowly and looked down in her eyes. "Lula," he breathed, "oh, you're wonderful. So small and so soft. Please, Lula! Please let me!"

"No, no, no," she stammered. "It ... it frightens me."

"There's nothing to be afraid of. I won't hurt you, honest, I won't."

"But ... but, it's such a ... a strange feeling."

"I know, I know, honey! But isn't it wonderful?"

She buried her face against his shoulder and did not say anything else until she felt his hand again, tentative, hesitant. Then she looked up at his face and in her agony of feeling and emotion whispered, "Please, don't."

"I won't go all the way, honey. Please let me teach you how wonderful it can be, even without going all the way."

His hand tugged gently at the top of her little panties and she lifted herself clear of the seat to make it easier for him. She clung to him, the tears running down her cheeks and into the corners of her mouth, her breath rasping in her throat.

Then he was on his knees before her and she was digging her fingers into his hair, throwing her head back and screaming with the searing agony of pleasure!

After that night, she had studiously avoided the boy who had been her partner in crime. It was not that she had anything against him. As a matter of fact, she was painfully attracted to him. It was not that she was suffering from any feeling of shame either. She looked back upon the experience with a deep, awesome kind of thrill. Just a fleeting thought of it was enough to make her throb all over again.

No. She had frightened herself. For a brief while she had looked deep into the cavernous depths of her own passion, and her capacity for that sort of enjoyment, and what she had seen was a violence that far surpassed both her years and her opportunities.

The boy, who had fallen deeply in love with her, was heartbroken, but she would have nothing to do with him. In fact, she had shut herself up within herself, avoiding all situations that might lead to a repetition of something she felt had been beyond control. She had felt a little vulgar. Yes, even a little cheap and "easy." She was afraid to let it happen again.

She had had plenty of opportunities in college, but she had managed to shy away from them all ...

But now, the hand that held hers tightened slightly and she became painfully aware of how strongly she was attracted to the young man sitting there by her side in the semi-darkness.

"A penny for your thoughts," he smiled. "There's a corny line for you."

"I was just being comfortable," she murmured, "I was thinking how good it feels, just sitting here, kind of feeling all this," she gestured vaguely about the tremendous space of the bricked-in backstage, "kind of letting it soak in."

"It's deceptive, isn't it?" said Luke. "It gets in your blood and you can't get away from it. Oh, for a real talent," he went on. "What I wouldn't give to really have what it takes."

She looked at him fondly. "You've got what it takes, Luke."

He glanced down and rubbed his hands over the baggy pants. "Yeah," he said bitterly, "baggy pants and a clown make-up. No, that's not what I'm talking about. I'm hungry, Lula. I'm so hungry I can feel the bile in my throat. I'm hungry for ... for stature. For the dignity that sometimes goes with real artistry. I fool myself into thinking that this is a stopgap. That some day I will be discovered. And deep down inside I know better. Who the hell is going to notice a jerk like me?"

She lifted his hand and pressed it against her cheek. "Don't talk like that, Luke, please. You have more talent in your little finger than ... than ..." She glanced helplessly around her. The illusion was gone. It was just the shabby, dirty area backstage of a burlesque house now ... "anybody in this theatre."

He smiled wryly. "That ain't saying much," he muttered.

She smiled encouragingly and said, "How old are you, Luke?"

"Twenty-four," he muttered glumly, "and time's a-wasting."

Now she laughed, a gay catch in the sound. "Why, Luke, you're just a child. You know enough about the theatre to know how often it takes years ... years and patience."

He looked at her adoringly. "Don't you ever think of yourself?" he asked. "You're always cheerful. You always have an encouraging word for me."

"Not always cheerful," she said a little sadly. "It's just that ... well, we're young. This is just a stopgap," she reminded him.

He suddenly bent and kissed her hand. "I think I'm falling in love with you," he said. Then he stood up abruptly. "Work, work," he smiled. "My public awaits me." He held her hand for a moment longer, then hurried off to his dressing room to get ready for his next appearance.

Lula sat there for a little while longer, feeling a clinging sadness that the illusion had been shattered, but also conscious of the disturbing stirring in her vitals which was the result of her strong attraction to the young comedian.

Just then the brasses in the pit indicated that the acrobatic dancer had come to her last triumphant contortion and two grimy stagehands hurrying toward the platform on which she sat reminded her that "Merma" was about to dunk her semi-nudity for the edification of the assembled multitude. She rose and went quickly to the chorus dressing room.

She found upon her arrival that most of the girls were already dressed in their revealing Latin-American rhumba costumes that served as background for Margot Diego's exotic disrobing. They were sitting around, playing solitaire, reading the paper and chatting.

She quickly threw off her terry-cloth robe and revealed herself, still dressed in the brief black and white checkered costume she had worn in the last chorus number.

She unzipped herself down the back and quickly pulled off the wispy outfit. She stood naked, except for her brief strippers' panties. As she reached for the top to her rhumba costume, the door to the dressing room opened and the chatter of the girls ceased in half-frightened awe.

Margot Diego had entered the room.

She was not dressed for her act yet, but wore a brilliant mandarin's robe which was very short and showed off to full advantage her long white tapering legs. She was smoking a cigaret. Her hair was hanging about her shoulders. She stood for a brief moment inside the door and regarded the room through half-lowered lids.

Finally her eyes landed on Lula.

She closed the door behind her and walked in. Lula hurriedly grabbed the top part of her costume from the peg on the wall and started to put it on, but Margot's hand on her arm stopped her.

"Just a minute, honey," she said softly and Lula stopped, frozen, with one hand still touching the costume in its place on the wall.

Margot turned her around slowly. The other girls were staring open-mouthed at this unashamed scene. A few giggled nervously, but no one spoke.

Lula's whole body turned pink with embarrassment. Her knees shook a little as she stood before the star stripper.

Margot looked her up and down and Lula felt an uncomfortable tightening of her breasts and loins as she became increasingly aware of the frankness of the stare.

"You're a good-looking little doll," said Margot, "maybe you'll be a menace to me before long." She smiled brightly, and tugging Lula slightly by the arm, she moved toward the door. "I'd like to talk to you for a minute."

Lula hung back. "What do you want?" she asked, her voice almost a whisper.

"I just want to talk to you for a minute."

"I can't go out there like this."

"Haven't you got a robe?"

"I've got to get dressed."

"You've got plenty of time. I'm not dressed either. You won't be needed if I'm not there."

"But the number is coming up soon."

"Oh, that tadpole out there has got to get through in her aquarium, and Luke and Little Jack have got their doctor skit to do. We've got plenty of time. Put your robe on and come along." She went to the door and waited imperiously.

Lula shrugged hesitantly into her robe again, this time with nothing under it except her tiny panties. Her breasts rubbed with pleasurable unpleasantness against the rough terry-cloth. The other girls were staring avidly at the little scene, throwing sidelong glances at each other, nodding their heads meaningfully.

Margot opened the door and Lula fled quickly through it. After the star stripper had closed the door, the chorus room exploded into a waterfall of nervous chatter, punctuated by sneering snickers. It sounded like a barnyard.

Lula stopped just outside the door. "What do you want?"

"Oh, don't be so haughty. Come on. I want to talk to you." And Margot led the way to her own private dressing room. She held the door open for Lula, then followed her in and closed it.

"Sit down. Have a cigarette?"

Lula shook her head mutely.

"Drink?"

Again Lula refused. "What do you want?" she asked, a little breathlessly.

Margot sat back against the dressing-table and allowed her short robe to swing open. She was wearing nothing but her tiny white G-string. "You're scared of me, aren't you?" she asked.

"No, I'm not," Lula insisted.

"Yes, you are. I don't know what you've heard about me, but I assure you that there's nothing to be scared of."

"I haven't heard anything about you."

"Then what are you scared of?"

Lula honestly did not quite know. She tried to answer with candor. "I'm not really scared. I don't know what it is."

"Suppose I tell you," Margot said, "the other day when you were leaving Hansel's office you ran into me, or rather we ran into each other. My hands *accidentally*," she emphasized the word, "touched you a couple of times and you think I'm on the make for you, don't you?"

Lula looked at her in bewilderment.

"Don't pretend you don't know what I'm talking about," Margot said wearily. "They all do. They look at you with great innocent eyes as if they'd never heard of such a thing. Honest to God, sometimes I want to puke!"

"I *don't* know what you're talking about."

Margot pulled erect from her slumping position against the dressing-table, her robe swung shut, and she walked slowly across the room to a screen, over which hung a number of costumes. Her fingers reached out and explored with exquisite sensuality the delicate materials. She spoke without looking at Lula.

"When you were very young, were you ever attracted to your teacher?"

Lula stared at her. Finally, she nodded dumbly.

"What did it feel like?" Margot asked.

Lula got up. "I'd better hurry or I won't be ready."

"Oh, sit down. We've got plenty of time. We're just talking. I want to get to know you. I liked you the minute I saw you. Please sit down." Margot swung back from the screen and sat down on the bench by the dressing-table. Lula sat in a straight-backed chair that stood almost in the center of the room. Margot opened a drawer and pulled out a little silver flask. She dumped a bit of the contents into two glasses and poured a little ice water from a pitcher on the table into each. She held one out to Lula.

"Come on, honey, have a little drink. I wish I could make you believe that I'm just trying to be friendly. Honestly, when I saw you in Hansel's office, I liked you at once. It's plain as anything that you're going to go places."

Lula reluctantly accepted the drink and sipped it cautiously, almost as if she were afraid that Margot had put something in it besides bourbon.

"Now," Margot said, "that's better. Please do believe me, honey, I've got no axe to grind. I'd just like to make friends. Do you believe me?"

Lula hesitated. "I guess I do," she finally said.

Margot's eyes filled with realistic tears. "I don't know why it is. Everybody is always scared of me. What can *I* do to anybody?" She wiped the tears from her eyes. "I don't know what it is about me … I've got a clean conscience. So I'm the star! So my name *is* in neon lights out on the marquee. Does that make me any different from you girls? Why won't anybody ever talk to me? Why won't they have anything to do with me?"

She blubbered a little and Lula, in all innocence, moved a little closer to her.

"Even the star can get lonely," Margot wept. "Oh, if you only knew how hard I've worked to get to the top. I had to deny myself all sorts of things. I had to be hard as nails. I had to walk on all kinds of nice people. But it was just to get to the top. It was just to realize my ambitions. Please! Be kind to me. Talk to me ... I am so lonely!"

Lula was appalled. The more she saw of the inside workings of the theatre, the more she was amazed. It was never like this in college. "I ... I'll be your friend, Margot."

The stripper suddenly was all smiles.

"Drink your drink, honey," she said. "Drink it and talk to me. Oh, gosh, I tell you, my life isn't all it might be. But I'm honest. I just wanted to get somewhere."

"I understand," said Lula, although she didn't quite.

"I knew you would, honey. The moment I saw you in Hansel's office I knew you would!"

Margot's hand reached out and fell lightly on Lula's knee. She felt like pulling back from the touch, but pity prompted her to stay in her position, painfully conscious of the warm palm that caressed her gently.

"What were we talking about?" said Margot brightly. "Oh, yes, I remember. It was about schoolteachers."

Lula nodded. She felt very strange. She wanted to be friendly with the older woman who so obviously wanted to be friendly with her, but the conversation seemed to take such intimate turns.

Margot went on. "I asked you if you hadn't ever felt attracted to a woman teacher and you nodded your head. I guess you must have meant yes."

Lula nodded again, wishing she were well out of the room and back in her own domain again. The chorus dressing room was not the most desirable place in the world, but it was infinitely better than this. She was still scared of Margot, but her fright was drowned out by compassion for this poor lonely woman, mixed with a vague apprehension that would not go away, no matter how hard she tried to subdue it.

"Yes," she faltered, "I meant yes."

"What did it feel like? Did you want her?"

"Want her?"

"Yes, I mean—did you want to touch her? To … to kiss her?"

Lula blushed. "I … I guess I did."

"Did the feeling scare you?"

"I … I guess so …"

"Don't you see? That's what I mean. In a way, because I'm older than you … because I'm ahead of you in the game, I kind of attract you … don't I?"

"Well … yes … I guess you do, in a way."

"I kind of scare you that way, don't I?"

Lula jumped to her feet. "I really must go."

Margot stood up slowly. "Wait," she said, "open your robe a minute, won't you, please? I want to see you."

Lula did not move.

"Please, please, I beg you, don't misunderstand me. I want to see you just so I can help you. We're in the same business, and I have so many more years of experience. I could help you. I really could."

"I don't want to stay permanently in this business."

"All the same, you *are* in it. Please let me help you. Let me see you so that I can help you display yourself better."

"I don't want to 'display' myself."

"Honest, honey, I don't mean anything bad about it. I just want to help you. Please, please open your robe."

Lula slowly let her robe fall open. Margot stepped behind her and lifted it from her shoulders. Lula stood practically naked before her.

Margot drew a deep breath and stepped back admiringly. "You're beautiful," she breathed. "You're the most beautiful thing I've ever seen."

Lula was trembling. She was terribly embarrassed and her soft, satiny skin was flushed to a deep pink. She wanted to run and hide. She wanted to crawl into the floor and pull the boards over her. How had she ever gotten into this situation?

Margot circled around her, admiring her from every angle. The soft curve of the small, slender hips, the taut, white, girlish thighs, the pert peaks of the domed breasts. She reached out a tentative hand and cupped one gently.

Lula jumped as if a snake had bitten her and grabbed her robe. "No, no!" she cried and pulled the terry-cloth tightly about her.

"I just can't keep my hands off you," stammered Margot. "You are so desirable. You're the most desirable thing I've ever seen."

"Oh, no! No! I've got to go," cried Lula and she started toward the door.

Margot sank into the chair by the dressing-table. "That's what I mean," she wept. "Everybody misunderstands me! I was just trying to be friendly. Please, please don't go out of here mad at me. I just wanted to help you. Please don't you misunderstand me, too."

The tears were running down her cheeks and Lula, despite her revulsion, felt sorry for the exotic stripper who seemed so lonely, so lost.

Pulling her robe closely about her, she stepped close to Margot and timidly touched her hair. "I'm sorry, Margot, I'm truly sorry. But ... but I've just got to go and change my costume."

She ran out of the room ...

Joe Pastelli was standing on the fly-floor, looking over the tops of the drapes at the big finale of his show. He was flicking an unlit cigarette from one side of his mouth to the other and his sharp, dark face wore an expression of pleasure. It had been four years since he had bought the Brunswick and gone into the burlesque business, much to the horror of his good and moral family.

"Aw," he had sighed to their objections, "what's the harm in a little sex as long as it pays off. We're all human …"

And with his shrewd understanding of what he called "sex" he had run the old shabby theatre into an extremely profitable business. True, the city was beginning to frown a little at the alleged immorality that took place on its burlesque stages, but Joe knew how to still such qualms. A little "gift" here, a little "present" there, a few passes discreetly pressed into the correct palms.

"After all, what's wrong with a few bare legs? They never hurt anybody. My shows are art. Let the frustrated old biddies who are married to my customers put that in their pipes and smoke it. They could learn a few things from my girls."

Now he smiled with satisfaction. His enterprise and discretion were paying off. Mama was installed in a brand new ten room house. Luigi was going to college, studying to be a great lawyer.

He himself was in possession of a luxurious establishment on the Drive. What if his suits were still a little sharp? What if the accents of his youth on the East Side were still on his tongue? What if the aroma of garlic still clung faintly to him? It was almost drowned out by expensive toilet water. He was having no trouble with the dames any longer. Any babe was glad to give him whatever he wanted. He could give something in return.

The finale was coming to its crashing climax with Little Jack Horner's unctuous voice coming over the p.a. system.

Little Jack Horner, a crumb, if Joe had ever seen one, but what an investment! He could sing, he could dance, he could take the narration on the p.a., he was a fine comedian. Four-in-one! What an investment! What if he did petrify the girls with his pinching, with his little pats and slaps? With his evil eyes? That redhead, his wife, who went on the stage by the name of Susie, but whose name backstage was Pee Wee, had him under control. Joe had been warned against employing him. But that had been two months ago and nothing untoward had happened yet. A good investment!

"Ladies and gentlemen, the Brunswick Theatre takes pleasure in bringing back for your approval the delectable girls of our show. First, the little girls of the chorus—give them a hand, folks, they deserve it!"

The eighteen conglomerate parcels of female flesh pranced on, swishing their little short skirts. The theatre thundered with applause and Joe Pastelli felt a strong current of pleasure coursing through him. Of pride.

"And here is Merma, the aquatic wonder of all the world. How about a big hand for Merma?" He droned on, phony cheerfulness oozing over the loudspeakers.

Three … four young women, flaunting their hips and the quiver of their breasts in their skimpy panels and bras … redheads, brunettes, blondes … some big, some small and pert. After each had entered and bumped a little into the first row and taken her place up center in front of the chorus leaving a space in their midst for the star, a howl of approval rose from the house and Joe had the pleasurable knowledge that he was doing well. Very well, indeed.

"And finally, ladies and gentlemen, the *star* of our show. The pride of the Brunswick, whose name echoes through all of Latin America! Ladies and gentlemen, we give you … MARGOT DIEGO!"

Margot strutted on, wearing nothing but her net bra and tiny white satin G-string. Margot, promenading down to the footlights, throwing kisses, grinding her lush torso. Backing up and striking a suggestive pose at the center of the stage, throwing her arms in the air as the curtains swept together and the audience howled and whistled and shouted.

Joe spit out his cigarette and turned in satisfaction to enter his little cluttered office off the fly-floor.

What a babe! She had really *made* the current edition of the follies! And she had sweetened Joe's life considerably. Holy smoke, what a capacity! For a little bit of everything. When she could get away from her husband, she really "fitted in" in the satin and chrome of the apartment on the Drive. Being nice to him, being nice to his friends. What a hunk of merchandise!

He was still sitting there, rolling a new cigarette in his mouth, musing on his success and being particularly pleased with himself, when Margot came in. She closed the door behind her and went to perch on his desk. She was wearing the Chinese mandarin's robe again, her legs gleaming and although it had only been a short time since she had gone through her strenuous act, not a hair was out of place, not a drop of perspiration on her creamy brow.

"Joey," she said softly.

He looked at her with evident pleasure and pride. "Baby," he said, "you were great today. Just great. I swear you've got the most artistic strip in the business. You really wow 'em!"

She lowered her eyes demurely. "Thank you," she whispered.

"I mean it," he went on vehemently. "You're terrific!"

She smiled prettily. "What is this?" she asked. "The weekly meeting of the mutual admiration society?"

"Well, honey, I'm a member as far as you are concerned."

She looked her gratitude. "I've got a new idea for the show, Joey," she said.

"Great," he answered, "any idea you have is OK by me. Anything you say."

"No, listen," she laughed, "I'm serious."

"So am I, baby, so am I."

"Well, look," she said briskly, "don't you think that fishbowl act is a little worn out?"

"Who? Merma?"

"Yes. It's such a wet mess."

"Aw, Merma is a good kid."

Margot looked at him closely. "What do you mean by that?"

He was startled. "Nothing. Nothing. Just that I think she's OK."

"Her act has about as much sex in it as the local YWCA swimming team."

"It has novelty."

"Novelty? So does a rhinoceros walking down Third Avenue. But has it got sex?"

"Now, wait a minute, Margot. Merma is not a rhinoceros."

"Have you looked at her lately? She's eating too damned much."

Joe searched his memory of the slim, athletic body of Merma, trying to recall as much as an ounce of fat on her. Try as he did, he could not. "What do you mean, she's fat? She's built like a boy."

"Well, is that good?" Margot asked triumphantly, with exquisite disregard for logic.

"I think she's doing fine."

"What's the matter with you?" she asked with elaborate disdain. "Are you blind? Or have you got the hots for her?"

Joe threw out his hands. "Listen, Margot! What're you trying to do? You've got me all confused."

"Well, there you see, you're not sure of her act at all."

Joe stared at the dark stripper helplessly. So help him, he would never grow up to the point where he could hold his own in an argument with a woman. There was something so slippery about such a conversation. One minute you thought you had a good firm grip on the point of the discussion and the next minute nothing made any sense at all.

"What are you trying to say?" he asked in abject surrender.

Margot moved around the desk to re-perch herself confidentially close to Joe. She leaned toward him and her robe fell away, disclosing her full firm breasts in their confining net brassiere. Joe's fingers itched to reach out and touch them, but he restrained himself. He sat back and waited for what was to come.

"Look, Joe," Margot purred. "Don't you think it is time for us to spring a new, hot thing on the audience? Merma is corny. Now, let's face it. Every nightclub in the country has got some babe taking it off under water. What the hell is sexy about that? The water isn't even cold enough to make their points rear up a little. It's just a wet mess, like I said. A woman can't look inviting while she's floundering around in six feet of water like a goldfish. You just sit there, waiting for her to grow fins. Why don't you dump Merma and get us something new and hot and different?"

"Like what, for instance? Merma is a good investment. The crowd likes her."

"I've thought an awful lot about that, Joe. All I care about is that we have a bang-up show. Now, how about introducing a brand new stripper? Somebody nobody has ever heard about before. Spring her like a bomb from a clear sky."

Joe stared at her in puzzlement. "Who?" he asked.

Margot was elaborately casual. "Oh, I don't know ... somebody new, that's all. Somebody fresh."

"Do you know of anybody?"

"Not anybody in particular. Oh, I could think of one or two who might be exciting, but then ..." cunningly, "I don't guess you're much for taking chances."

Joe's masculine gambling instinct was stung by that. His courage as a daring businessman was questioned. He rose to the occasion. "What do you mean I won't take a chance? I'll take a chance as fast as the next fellow. Faster! What do you think I've been doing with the Brunswick for the last four years? Playing safe all the time? You don't get nowhere playing safe!"

"Now you're talking, Joe! That was just what I wanted you to suggest. That we take a chance! Who shall we take a chance on?"

The "we" was not escaping Joe, but, instead of annoying him it flattered him a little that this exotic girl took such an interest in his business. He felt as if it were indeed he who had made the suggestion that a change was needed and that "they" take a chance. "I'd better look around a little," he said. "Maybe Hansel has got somebody up his sleeve."

This was the moment Margot had so carefully worked toward. "Do you agree with me, Joe?" she asked with a great show of girlish excitement. "Don't you think that a brand new figure would be a good addition to the show? Don't you?"

The suggestion had taken hold of Joe. A new face! A new figure! Somebody the crowd had never seen before. Spring it on them like a bomb from a clear sky. Big publicity spread. "Never before seen on any stage!" Fresh, young, exciting! What an idea! Honest, that Margot was worth her weight in gold! He must get her a little something to show his appreciation. What the hell was Merma? Just a fish, that was all. A fish! A wet blanket on the show! He chuckled to himself. What a wit! He could see it so clearly now. What they needed was a good solid touch of freshness.

He spoke with enthusiasm. "You're right, Margot! That's what we need all right. Here," he reached for the phone, "I'll get on it right now and see what we can drum up."

"Wait a minute, Joe." She sounded like a modest young girl, unsure of herself and inadequate before the superior brains and initiative of a big strong man. "Would you … could I make a suggestion?"

Joe looked at her fondly. "Of course you can! I hope to tell you!"

"Well, there's a girl right here … in the chorus."

"Here? In my chorus? Who?"

"Her name is Lula Lang."

"You mean that new chicken? Came in a couple of days ago?"

"That's the one."

"But she's just a kid. She hasn't got any experience at all."

"Isn't that just what we want? You've got me for hot experience. She would add a touch of innocence."

A brilliant idea! Joe could see it now. The contrast between the two women! The passionate hotblooded boldness of Margot, flinging herself in open invitation about the stage. Dark, raven-haired. And Lula Lang, small, blonde, demure, even embarrassed like a young bride, blushing as she reluctantly removed her clothes. This was hot! This was greatness! Why hadn't he thought of such a thing before? Lula early in the show, promising, teasing. Margot fulfilling the promise. This was terrific! What a killing could be made from such a combination ...

"That's great, Margot! That's stupendous! Let's get her up here right away!" Suddenly he stopped. "What about her? Will she be interested?"

"She'll play coy, Joe. She's new in the business. But ... don't take no for an answer. *Make* her do it! We can become the greatest show in town. Don't let anything stand in your way."

"OK. Let's get her up here."

"I don't want to be here when you talk to her, Joe. She wouldn't like my interfering. But don't let her refuse. Think what it will do for the show."

"Damned right, Margot! Don't you worry. She'll do what I want or she'll be without a job. I'll take care of that!"

He reached for the housephone and Margot, throwing him one last look which was met by an admiring wink from him, went out to return to her dressing room and await developments.

Maybe this would loosen up that little iceberg. Maybe this would stop her from being such a timid infant!

CHAPTER FOUR

The Brunswick went on. No soft hunger, no churning passion from within could stop the inexorable wave of entertainment.

(The scene is a doctor's office. The luscious Redhead, dressed in an almost transparent nurse's uniform is bustling around. At center is a table, a straight chair on either side. Enter the doctor. It is Luke Lucas. He is wearing a white coat, many times too big for him; around his neck hangs a monstrosity of a stethoscope that reaches almost to the floor. It hangs there obscenely, between his legs, dangling every time he moves. Out of his pockets stick all sorts of horrible instruments, saws, hammers, a drill. He is wearing a bushy wig that looks as if he had just emerged from a windtunnel.)

LUKE: Nurse, nurse!

REDHEAD: Yes?

LUKE: Oh, nurse, I want you to watch out for something this morning. My invention is arriving by express.

REDHEAD: Your invention?

LUKE: Yes. My invention.

REDHEAD: What sort of invention is it?

LUKE: Well, it's a new way of getting rid of disease by transference.

REDHEAD: By what?

LUKE: Transference. The invention transfers the disease from the patient, through electronic impulse to a dummy.

REDHEAD: But what will you do when *you* have the disease?

LUKE: I?

REDHEAD: Yes, didn't you say a dummy?

LUKE: That's not funny, nurse. (*Two "Express Men" enter from left stage, carrying a huge box between them.*) Ah, here we are! Set it down by the table, men, and help me unpack it. (*The "Express Men" set the box down by the table, open it and extract a complicated looking contraption, the front of which is covered with dials and flashing lights. They set it on the table and go out the same way they came in. Luke displays two handles at the ends of electric cords, one fastened on either side of the box.*)

LUKE: Now, you see here? You place the patient in this chair and put this handle in his hand. Then you put the dummy in this other chair and put this handle in its hand. Then you turn this switch and twist this dial and the disease is transferred from the patient to the dummy. The patient gets up and walks away completely healed.

REDHEAD: Why, that's wonderful! But where's the dummy?

LUKE: The man from the waxworks is bringing it over this morning. When it gets here, you be sure and call me so that we can try it out on some of today's patients.

(*He goes out at right stage and the Redhead fiddles with the machine a little bit. Some of the lights flash on and off and a loud buzzing is heard. The Redhead jumps violently. Little Jack comes hurrying in from left stage. She turns the machine off. Little Jack is dressed in a checkered suit of loud plaid. He is wearing a tiny derby, perched on top of a long black wig. His nose is scarlet.*)

JACK: Well, honey, here I am! Let's get going on our date!

REDHEAD: Oh, Jack, I'm sorry. I can't go with you today. The doctor is trying out a new experiment and he asked me specially to stay.

JACK: Now look, honey, you promised me! I've got a case of beer in the car and my hotdog … I mean the hotdogs are all ready and waiting. Come on. (*He tugs at the Redhead.*)

REDHEAD: No, Jack, I'm sorry, but I can't. And you get out of here now. You know how the doctor feels about my boy friend coming to see me during working hours. He'll fire me if he finds you here.

JACK: Honey, you swore you'd come.

REDHEAD: Well, I can't, so please go now. The doctor might come in at any moment.

JACK: Aw, the hell with him! I ain't scared of no sawbones.

REDHEAD: He'll fire me if he finds you here. And he'll murder you!

JACK: (*Makes an obscene movement toward right stage*) Nuts to him!

(*Just then Luke comes in hurriedly and Jack jumps to the chair at the left side of the table, trying to hide behind the machine. The Redhead is agitated. Luke comes to the table.*)

LUKE: Well, well, well, I see that the dummy has arrived. (*He peers intently at Jack, who fidgets nervously in his chair.*) Isn't it lifelike? (*Luke lifts the derby and runs his hand over Jack's hair.*) Isn't it sort of cute? (*He replaces the derby and runs a hand down over Jack's chest and stomach.*) Um … really looks good. If only it wasn't so stupid-looking. (*Jack is indignant, but Luke turns away.*) Now, if we can only get a patient, we'll see how the machine works. Oh. (*He laughs indulgently and pats Jack again.*) That poor old dummy will get all sorts of diseases, but then of course, it won't make any difference to it. (*A man comes in at left stage.*) Aha! Here's our first patient! (*The man is scratching prodigiously.*) And what can I do for you, my good man?

MAN: Oh, doctor, you *must* help me. (*He scratches.*) I've got the most awful itch! (*He scratches.*) All over. It's driving me crazy!

LUKE: Um-hmmm! I see. Well, my good man, you sit right down here (*Indicating right chair.*) and we'll see what we can do. (*The man sits and Luke puts the conductor into his hand. He puts the other conductor in Jack's hand and turns on the machine. It buzzes loudly and the lights flash on and off. The two men with the handles jump and squirm and tremble. After a moment Luke turns it off again.*) Now, how do you feel?

MAN: (*Standing up tentatively*) Why ... why ... I feel wonderful! It's all gone! Why you're a miracle worker! I'm going to go and tell all my friends! (*He rushes out.*)

LUKE: (*Rubbing his hands together*) It works! It works! I'll get famous! now, nurse, I'll be in my laboratory. If any other patients come in, you call me. (*He goes out.*)

JACK: (*Leaping up*) Come on, let's ... (*He stops in amazement and scratches his chest.*) What the hell is this? (*He begins to scratch madly all over.*) Come on, let's get out of here. (*He scratches insanely.*)

(*A man enters from left stage. Just at that moment Luke comes in again and Jack makes a dash for his chair.*)

LUKE: Well, well, here's another. Why didn't you call me, nurse? What can I do for you?

MAN: (*Stuttering*) I ... I ... I hea ... hea ...

LUKE: (*Helpfully*) Heard?

MAN: (*Explosively*) Have been told, that yu ... yu ... yu ...

LUKE: (*Helpfully*) I?

MAN: (*Explosively*) You!

LUKE: Me?

MAN: Yes! Can cu ... cu ... cu ...

LUKE: Cure?

MAN: Fix anything up.

LUKE: (*With pride*) Well, I don't know about that. I do my best.

MAN: Well, I stut ... stut ... stut ...

LUKE: Stutter?

MAN: Have a speech condition.

LUKE: (*Drily*) So I notice. Well, come here and sit down. (*Same business with conductors, switches and dials;*

the two men jump and squirm.) Now then. (*He turns machine off.*) How do you feel?

MAN: (*Stands up*) I … I … I feel great. It's all gone! I'll hurry and tell all my friends! (*He rushes out.*)

LUKE: (*As he leaves the stage*) Don't forget to call me when the next one comes.

JACK: (*Jumping to his feet*) For … for … for God's sa … sa … sa … Oh, lis … lis … lis … (*He scratches madly and sputters futilely. The Redhead looks at him in horror. A Swish enters from left. Luke comes in from right.*)

LUKE: Ah, here's another one. (*Jack dashes for his chair, but gets tangled up with the Swish, who seems to enjoy the entanglement. Finally Jack makes it.*) What can I do for you? (*The Swish prances over to Luke, looking him up and down.*)

SWISH: Well, all my friendth thaid I should come and thee you. They thaid you were jutht the nithest man. They thaid you could fix me up.

LUKE: Fix you up?

SWISH: Yeth. I alwayth feel tho queer. (*He giggles.*)

LUKE: I'll bet you do. Come here and sit down. (*He hands the Swish one of the conductors.*)

SWISH: Oh, thith ith nithe! (*He squirms a little in his seat.*)

LUKE: And here, now, we put the other conductor in the dummy's hand.

(*Jack resists, but finally has to hold the conductor. Luke turns on the machine. The Swish seems to be thoroughly enjoying himself. His hand is jumping and he is clinging with all his might to that nice conductor. Luke turns the machine off.*)
SWISH: Oh, pleathe, doctor, do it a little more.
(*Luke looks at him and shakes his head. He turns the machine on again and the two men jump and squirm. Finally Luke turns it off.*)
LUKE: Well, how do you feel?

SWISH: (*Jumping up*) Oh, I feel just fine, doctor. You are a miracle man! (*He starts after the Redhead, who flees out of his way.*) Oh, boy, do I feel great! I'm going to go and find me a girl! (*He rushes out.*)

LUKE: (*Laughs and leaves the stage.*)

JACK: (*Gets up slowly and lasciviously. He strikes a sexy pose, still scratching, but languidly now.*) Oh, thhucks, I fee ... fee ... feel ter ... ter ... ter ... terrible! Pleathe ... I've jutht got to ... to ... to ... get ou ... ou ... out of here! (*Swinging his hips and holding one hand behind his head, like a strutting woman, he starts out left. A woman comes rushing in.*)

WOMAN: Doctor! Doctor!

(*Luke comes in hurriedly.*)

LUKE: Yes? Yes? What is your trouble?

(*Jack dashes for the chair again.*)

WOMAN: Oh, doctor, I'm going to have a baby!

JACK: OH, NO! (*He falls fainting from his chair.*)

(BLACKOUT)

Lula stood on the sidewalk outside the stage entrance to the Brunswick Theatre. She was reading a letter from her mother.

Joe Pastelli had called her up to his office. He had looked her over with an interest which she had not been able to understand. Finally he had offered her, with a great show of generosity, a spot in the show as a stripper. She had refused and he had insisted. He had tried flattery. He had tried cajolery. Finally she had asked him why he wanted her to do this so badly. He had gone into an enthusiastic accolade about his own show and an idea he had had about an "innocent" strip, as he had called it. When she had still refused, he had become angry and had given her, finally, her choice between stripping or being fired.

She had been unhappy about it, but she had chosen the latter. The experience with Hansel was still fresh in her mind. The skimpy costumes she wore in the chorus embarrassed her dreadfully, but they were certainly not as bad as almost total nakedness would be. The very idea of stripping terrified and humiliated her. She could never bring herself to it. That was not what she had gone to college and spent her parents' money for. She would not even consider it.

She had gone down the stairs from the fly-floor with tears in her eyes, had dressed and packed her few belongings in a small paper parcel, avoiding any direct answer to the excited queries of the other girls.

On her way out of the theatre, the doorman had given her the letter from her mother. More to occupy her troubled mind with something besides her worries than for any other reason, she had stopped outside on the sidewalk, torn open the envelope and started to read the letter.

Dearest Lula,

I can not tell you how thrilled your father and I were to hear that you have finally gotten your foot in the door! I rushed right over to Mrs. Hoffstickler to tell her the good news and she got right on the phone and called Clara and your aunt Nita. Now the whole town knows about it, of course, and everybody is terribly excited. When I went down to the grocery this morning, Mr. Kraft, you know, the butcher, couldn't talk about anything else. They all expect so much of you and now that you are beginning to prove worthy of such great trust, they can hardly wait to see your name in the paper. Maybe you might even get into the movies and we could see you acting on the screen.

Your father is not doing as well as he might, but the good news about you gave him a real lift. Little Lula, I hesitate to mention this, but when we were sending you to school, your father and I spent most of our savings and things are a little pinched for us now. Do you think, now that you are working, that you might be able to help us a little now and again?

All your friends send their heartiest congratulations and your father sends his fondest love. Kisses to my soon-to-be-famous actress daughter.

Mother

Lula raised her head, but her tear-blurred eyes did not see the sunny street.

Then she turned and went back into the theatre.

At nine o'clock that evening Frank Powell left Tito's Restaurant and crossed the street to the Brunswick Theatre. He went around to the stage entrance. After he was inside, he went directly to Margot's dressing room. The exotic stripper was at her dressing-table, repairing her make-up. She smiled in the mirror at her handsome husband and nodded toward a chair. Frank sat down and stretched out his legs.

"What's on your mind, Margot? Tito gave me your message to come by here when I stopped in over there."

Margot finished putting lipstick on her mouth and turned in her stool to regard her husband. From a woman's viewpoint he was well worth looking at. Tall, distinguished, dark, with silver-grey streaks in his hair, Frank Powell was a catch, and Margot congratulated herself on how well she had done. He was the town's most sought after nightclub columnist and his column, "News From the Night," written in a crisp, sophisticated, humor-ous vein, was studied with avidity in thousands of homes every morning. The column was syndicated and appeared in dozens of papers all over the country. Through it, readers from Fresno to Philadelphia and from Portland to New Orleans caught a whiff of the exciting atmosphere of show business.

Since Margot's career depended on being constantly in the public eye, she could not have made a better marriage for herself. Besides which, simply as a person, Frank was not hard to take. He was witty, suave. A kindly man and a man of many and diverse interests. Some of these interests contributed to his fame, but there were others which he kept carefully hidden. Margot knew about them and understood how to use them in such a manner that she tied him to her with bonds that could not be broken.

Frank Powell was not necessarily what one might call a happy man. There were temptations which he hated, but which he could not resist. After succumbing to such weaknesses, he would castigate himself for days afterwards. Although he was bound to his wife with unbreakable ties, there were times when he loathed her, for he knew only too well that she traded on his weaknesses. Sometimes he hated her for imprisoning him in a cage, the bars of which were formed of her capacities as a fulfiller of his desires. Sometimes, when she was in the very act of fulfilling them, he hated her for the vulgar coarseness with which she did it. The deliberateness and the coldblooded vulgarity. But he always came back for more. She held him in an evil bondage.

Now she looked at him and smiled fondly. He shuddered a little, for he knew that one of her talents was the ability to seem at all times utterly innocent of guile and wickedness. He felt surer of himself with her when she was in one of her moods of outright coarseness.

"What have you been doing, honey?" she asked, making her voice sound like the voice of a young girl asking her boy friend where he had been keeping himself for so long.

"Just going my rounds," he answered a little warily.

"Are you awfully busy tonight?"

Frank pricked up his ears. That question was generally the introduction to her proposal that an evening be spent indulging their fancies.

"Not particularly," he said, "I'm a column ahead. What's on your mind?"

"Why don't you go out front and see the show? There's somebody in it tonight that I think you might like."

Frank felt the ancient stirring in his loins, the old pulsing of his blood. He felt vaguely repulsed by the sensation, but he could not have stopped now even if he had wanted to try. "Who?" he asked.

Margot smiled. She knew what this was doing to Frank. She knew how much the promise meant to him, how much the suspense and the anticipation meant. Frank had one of the richest imaginations she had ever encountered, and the expectation was in some ways more important and satisfactory to him than the final fulfillment. It took so little to start him off.

"A little blonde," she said, "Lula Lang. She's stripping for the first time tonight. I thought you might enjoy watching her. She's a little uncomfortable at the idea." She watched Frank's face twitch slightly and she smiled inwardly. What a child he really was. What a little Peeping Tom.

"Anything ..." he hesitated slightly, "anything doing?"

"Could be," she answered. "I have every intention of trying. You go out and see how you like her."

Frank nodded and went out and Margot smiled in satisfaction and anticipation.

"Ladies and gentlemen, it gives me real pleasure to introduce to you our producer, Mr. Joe Pastelli, who has an important message for you. Mr. Pastelli."

The audience stirred expectantly as Joe strode on stage in his dapper suit, his face wreathed in smiles. He gazed fondly at the assembled multitude.

"Ladies and gentlemen," he began, the East Side obvious in his speech, "I know how unusual it is that a producer steps in front of the curtain, but I have what I consider good news for you. In just a few moments you are about to witness the debut of a young lady whom the management of the Brunswick Theatre hopes will become a new and shining star in the firmament of burlesque. As yet very young and untried, this charming lady shows great promise. I believe that you will enjoy her innocence. We might say," and here he winked broadly at the audience, "that it is 'innocence in a broad' here at the Brunswick tonight."

He waited appreciatively for the giggle to subside in the audience before he went on. "Ladies and gentlemen, for the first time on any stage in the world, the Brunswick Theatre gives you this delectable young morsel, this tantalizing child … *Miss Lula Lang!*"

He made a broad gesture toward the center of the act curtain and Lula hesitantly stepped through and into the circle of golden light which was there waiting for her from the follow-spot.

Joe turned back to the audience and grinned broadly. "Ain't she a honey?" Then he left the stage and Lula was alone out there.

She was indeed a honey!

In keeping with the character of innocence demanded by Joe Pastelli, the wardrobe mistress had done herself proud. She had deliberately dressed Lula like a bride.

And now the small blonde stood there and the audience roared its approval of what it saw. She was dressed in a white lace floor-length dress with a small train that dragged behind her as she moved, barely showing now and again the dainty tips of high heeled white shoes. Her arms from the elbows down, were encased in white lace gloves that allowed her pink skin to shine through the mesh. Her blonde hair, in little-girl style, hung down in a cascade over her shoulders which were revealed by the gown. Draped over her hair and hiding her face almost entirely was a white bridal veil. The costume was exciting and somehow almost blasphemous at the same time. It was an invitation to partake of innocence, and an insult to that very innocence.

Lula sensed the hot flood of the men's approval pour over her and she felt their anticipation. It almost frightened the wits out of her. Her stomach turned, her heart pounded, and her knees and hands trembled uncontrollably. She stood rooted to the spot where she had first appeared.

Eventually the applause died out and the theatre was shrouded in breathless silence while the men waited to see what she would do next.

She did nothing. She simply stood there, her head turning slightly from side to side as if she were looking for an avenue of escape.

Joe Pastelli was raging in the wings. "Come on!" he whispered frantically. "Get going!" Margot, who was standing beside him, smiled at the girl's discomfiture. She craned her neck slightly and tried to see if she could make out Frank's figure in the box next to the stage. But she could not see him.

Frank was there, however. He was standing in the dark rear of the box, his eyes glued to the small blonde down on the stage. He was painfully aware that amazing things were happening to him. Never in all his life had he seen so beautiful a girl. To him she was the most exquisite thing he had ever laid eyes on. He pressed his back against the rear wall of the box, as if the strong pressure could somehow ease the violence of the emotions flooding through him. It did no good. He could not stand still. He shuffled his feet and drew in deep breaths of air. But his lungs would not fill properly. His whole body felt as if it were pulsing with the frantic beats of his heart.

He *had* to know this girl. He had to know her *well!*

Finally Joe Pastelli's desperate urging reached Lula's ears. She stirred painfully and walked slowly toward the left of the stage, as far away from the tense whisper as she could get. Here she stopped again, and the audience, slowly becoming aware of her embarrassment, began to urge her on. She heard the crude suggestions from the men in the house as if they were reaching her through the murmur of a little waterfall. Her eyes were half closed and her ears seemed to be filled with cotton.

She was blushing so furiously that her upper arms glowed pink in the golden light. She was hardly aware of the gentle sound of the soft music coming from the orchestra. Since she was not aware of it, her movements were not in rhythm to it. She gave, to the unknowing spectator, an impression of lost, bewildered virginity, faced for the first time with crude, harsh life.

The urging from the audience finally set her in motion again. She moved toward the center of the stage, and knowing with a sick feeling that she could not stall any longer, she tremblingly began to remove her gloves.

The audience howled.

She could not see how she could go on with this violation of her own person. Every part of the structure of her upbringing, every tiny bit of her background, every fiber in her innate modesty was protesting within her.

But both gloves came off and were dropped listlessly on the floor. By now she was close to the right side of the stage and Joe's voice was insistent in her ears. "Come on! Come on! Get going!"

Margot nudged the producer with her elbow. "Leave her alone," she whispered, choking down her contemptuous laughter for the cringing girl. "This ineptness is her biggest stock in trade. There isn't a man out there who isn't enjoying the delicious feeling that he is violating a virgin. Leave her alone!"

Joe stopped calling to Lula and stood there, chewing his cigarette nervously, impatiently awaiting the outcome.

It made no difference to Lula whether he was whispering or not. By now she was so frightened that nothing made any difference. The urging of the men in the audience was like the slowly approaching growl of a big wild beast intent on devouring her. All she could think of was escape.

With a sudden wild jerk, she tore the zipper down the front of her gown, and stumbling out of it as it cascaded about her feet she ran blindly from the stage.

Once off, she kept running … right into the arms of Joe. "Get back out there, you little dope!" he whispered hoarsely, "you've got them eating out of your hand. Listen to them!"

She was dimly aware of a howling, whistling, screeching roar, that washed and eddied over her senses like breakers in the ocean over the head of a drowning man.

"No! No! No!" she cried, her hands clawing wildly at him. "Let me go! Let me go!"

But Joe held her tightly, pulling and tugging her toward the stage. She fought him every inch of the way, while Margot watched, her whole figure a symbol of gloating.

Then they were at the edge of the stage and Lula suddenly felt herself propelled violently forward and found herself again in the center of the golden light that had been waiting for her.

By now the wings were filled with members of the company watching Lula's reluctance with varying degrees and kinds of emotion, among them Luke, his teeth grinding with anger.

When Frank, hidden in the darkness of the box, saw the girl's white figure emerging so abruptly from the wings, he took a quick step forward. Then he pulled himself back again with an effort and pressed against the wall. His mouth was open and his breath was coming fast. But mingled with the stirring of his senses was a growing feeling of compassion, of pity for this frail, blonde thing, which seemed to be ravished before his eyes.

At any other time the pose struck by Lula as she found herself in the center of the light once more would have been ludicrous. With her arms and hands, and by pressing her legs together, she tried desperately to hide her comparative nudity, to protect her wildly protesting modesty.

The men in the audience roared their approval. Everything Lula did seemed to them to be part of a fantastically cleverly characterized strip. A strip such as they had never seen before. Every cringe of the stunningly beautiful girl, every frantic attempt to protect herself came to them as wonderfully subtle parts of a rapidly growing suspense, apparently deliberately attained through the dramatic talent of the stripper.

In her tiny bra and strippers' panels Lula was unbelievably beautiful. Both were white satin. The bra was almost covered by the veil which still hid her head and face, but the panels could not conceal her long white legs which were revealed from hips to ankles for the approval of the goggling, roaring men in the audience.

Joe Pastelli could contain himself no longer. "Bump!" he cried over the uproar. "Bump, damn it! Bump! Or I'll throw you out in the street the minute you come off that stage! Bump!"

Lula, almost blinded by her tears, painfully conscious of the sweat of fear that was pouring down her sides, stumbled clumsily toward the center of the stage. Her skin crawled with loathing for herself and her stomach felt like a heaving, crunching lump of clay when she finally rolled her hips. The movement was so slight that it was almost imperceptible, but its very slightness was its biggest virtue. In the audience men roared their approval, looked slyly sideways at each other, stirred restlessly in their seats. This was an experience none of them would forget for a long, long time.

Lula was crying openly now as she stumbled from side to side of the stage, helplessly rolling her hips a little here and jerking them a little there, her long legs flashing, her diaphragm heaving with her sobs.

Joe yelled at her, his voice coming thinly to her through the din. "Get that bra off! Get it off!"

She reached up, and without bothering with hooks or snaps tore the bra from where it was lodged around her ribs and revealed herself with only the bridal veil covering her tiny trembling breasts.

The yell from the house was like a physical blow to her and it seemed to be this physical thrust that flung her off the stage, again into the arms of Pastelli who was laughing and cursing at the same time. "Wow, girl! You're a sensation! Listen at them!"

She felt herself jerked from Joe's arms and became dimly aware of Luke's pitying face above her. She heard Luke speak and was startled to find that he was crying, "That's enough! That's enough! Let her go. Can't you see what this is doing to her?"

Joe raged. "Turn her loose!"

But Luke held her fast. Then she realized that she was free again and saw through her tears Luke struggling in the hands of a couple of husky stagehands who had come running at Joe's call. Joe was holding her by the arms, shaking her, yelling in her ear. "You've still got the panels to go! Get in there and get them off! Go on!" Her breasts were trembling with the violence of his shaking and she felt naked. Naked as she had never known it was possible to feel. Again she tried to defend herself, but she could not handle Joe. The last she saw before she was pushed onstage were the leering eyes of Margot, washing over her body, touching her, caressing her. She felt, as she stood again in the circle of light and heard the quickened tempo of the music and the insistent raving of the audience as if she were a livid mass of crawling sickness. All she could think about was to get it over with, and now laughing crazily through her sobs she flung herself across the stage, jerking and grinding, her veil and hair flying wildly, sweat dripping from her sides, her knees wobbling drunkenly.

Frank, in the box, clenched his hands in mad fury. His pounding heart reached out to the girl and everything in him cried, "Stop! Stop it!"

It was as if Lula had suddenly gone insane. Her body which had cringed before, now flung itself in desperate arched abandon across the stage floor. Her hands thrashed graspingly through the air and her sobbing laughter rang through the house which was suddenly deadly silent, as if the men assembled there realized that they were witnesses to something grand and wild and mad, as if they were confronted with a level of passionate experience which they, with their little middle-class souls and senses would never have been capable of experiencing, had it not been for this wonderful girl.

And the final moment came. In the center of the stage, Lula ripped the panels from her waist and stood there for one trembling second, naked except for the veil and a tiny G-string. The effect was as of a maddening aphrodisiac on the men in the audience.

As Lula flung herself, sobbing, on the floor and the curtains swept closed, the house went wild. They roared and clapped and whistled and threatened to tear the theatre apart. Ten times the curtains swept open and closed again. Lula did not move. She lay in the center of the floor, her body doubled up in futile self-protection. She was weeping hysterically.

During the uproar, Frank left the box and the theatre. For a long time he stood blindly on the street outside, then he stumbled across to Tito's Restaurant and began drinking.

Margot stood in the wings watching Joe going to the prostrate form of Lula, picking her up and carrying her, still sobbing violently, off the stage. Her eyes followed the man and his burden as he carried her up the stairs and into his office.

Her mind was a seething whirlpool of mixed emotions. She had instigated this strip in order to break Lula down. She had never imagined that it would be anything but a flop. Now the front curtain kept opening and closing in her mind. The enthusiastic ovation from the house kept ringing in her ears and Margot had to ask herself whether she had been very smart in starting this. She had had no intention of allowing Lula to outshine her own act. But it appeared that the novice had been a bigger hit with the audience than Margot had ever been. Her stardom was in danger and Margot decided that something would have to be done about it.

As the comedians frolicked onto the stage for the next act, she turned and followed Joe and Lula up to the office on the fly-floor. When she opened the door, she saw Lula lying on the old battered leather couch. She was covered with a blanket and Joe was leaning over her. The blonde girl's sobs had subsided and Joe was talking softly to her.

"You were marvellous, honey. You wowed them! I've never had such a success in my life! We'll really slay them together!"

Lula whispered, "I'll never do it again. Never. I was just *sick* inside!"

"You can't stop now, honey. You're the biggest thing that ever happened to burlesque! You can't quit now. They'll be yelling for you!"

"Oh, no! No!" She turned her face to the wall and started crying again.

Margot leaned against the door-frame. "What a pretty picture! Outraged modesty sobbing its heart out."

Joe turned to her enthusiastically. "Margot, I've never been so keyed-up in my life! It was the most exciting thing I ever watched."

Margot's mouth twisted slightly. "Yeah, I know, that's what you said to me."

"Oh listen, Margot, I don't mean that you're outclassed! You know I don't mean that! But, holy crutches, what a combination the two of you will make. Everything I dreamed about when I made that suggestion that Lula strip!"

Margot smiled wryly. So now it was entirely Joe's idea.

Joe went on, "I'll build the whole show around you two. Innocence and experience. What a combination! There isn't another show in town with such a punch. We'll pack 'em in."

Margot's eyes narrowed. "Do you mean that I'm going to be sharing my billing with *her?*" She put contemptuous emphasis on the final word.

"What's wrong with that? You won't lose your star billing. You'll be in the greatest show in the city, one of the stars."

"*One* of the stars," Margot said, her mouth twisting.

Joe didn't hear her. "I'll do the whole show over. I'll build the whole thing up from scratch." He turned and looked at the girl on the couch. "What an act! What a girl!"

Margot turned and went out. She moved slowly to her dressing room and sat down by the mirror. For a long time she regarded herself with something less than pleasure. "Smart, aren't you?" she asked herself with distaste. "You were going to teach that little tease a lesson, weren't you? Well, the damn thing has boomeranged on you." Then she smiled a little slyly. "Well, at least it may have waked her up. We'll wait and see. Wait and see."

She removed the mandarin's robe from her sleek body and began vigorously applying powder from an enormous puff, to her full breasts. Her act was coming up. She had competition now. Margot was not used to competition. Instead of discouraging her, it spurred her on. She would show that little tease. She had plans for her. Big plans ...

She wondered how Frank had liked Lula and her body tingled pleasurably as she wondered.

After three double Scotches Frank went into Tito's office back of the restaurant. He borrowed the restaurant owner's old battered typewriter, and while the liquor was in his blood and Lula was pounding in his loins he wrote the most glowing review he had ever written in his life. He was enchanted with the girl and his review said so. Her name echoed and re-echoed through the lines of his column. Who was she? Who was this startling blonde that went by the name of Lula Lang?

When he had finished, he called his office and told them to scrap tomorrow's column. He was bringing a much hotter one right over.

A few days later the column appeared in Lula's hometown.

CHAPTER FIVE

They licked their lips and leered lasciviously. From all walks of life they came—bankers, brokers, carpenters, stokers. They paid their fee and demanded to be relieved of the cares of the day. Flesh—gleaming pink and white female flesh—was their demanded remedy.

(STREET SCENE)

(*Luke comes in from stage right. He is nattily dressed in a lavender suit and a large ten-gallon white hat. He is wearing a flowing bow tie. He is met by Little Jack Horner coming in from stage left. Little Jack is dressed as a caricature of an explorer. He has a checked suit with a long cape on. On his head is a Sherlock Holmes cap. He is smoking a long pipe that hangs to his knees and is sporting a huge red beard. His pants are plus-fours.*)

LUKE: Jack! Little Jack! Where have you been? It's ages since I've seen you!
JACK: (*Pompous voice*) Oh, I've been exploring.
LUKE: Exploring?
JACK: Yes, old man. I've been in the wilds of Tibet.
LUKE: Tibet?
JACK: That's right.

LUKE: Ti-bet you, you haven't! (*He slaps his knee, guffaws and leers at the audience.*)

JACK: I may get sick.

LUKE: Have you really been to Tibet?

JACK: I sure have. I brought back some fascinating things.

LUKE: What?

JACK: Well, I brought back a woman with three coccyxes.

LUKE: No?

JACK: Yes.

LUKE: What does she do with them?

JACK: She sits on them.

LUKE: No?

JACK: Yes. What would you do, if you had three coccyxes?

LUKE: (*Leering at the audience*) I would find me a beautiful girl and have *her* sit on them.

JACK: She wouldn't be able to.

LUKE: You don't know the girls in this town. What else did you bring back?

JACK: I brought a love philter.

LUKE: A love … what?

JACK: Philter! Philter!

LUKE: When did they start having to filter that?

JACK: No, no! It's for inhalation.

LUKE: For … ? How do you do that?

JACK: (*Taking a small vial from his pocket*) This is it.

LUKE: This little old thing?

JACK: That's right. All you have to do is wave this under the nose of a young lady and she'll do anything you ask her to.

LUKE: Anything?

JACK: Absolutely. (*He starts to put the vial back in his pocket.*)

LUKE: Not so fast! Not so fast! Let me see it. (*Jack hands it to him.*) You mean that all you have to do is wave this under a girl's nose and she'll do anything? Anything?

JACK: That's what I said.

LUKE: (*Jumping up and down*) Oh boy! Oh boy! (*Turning and staring at Jack.*) I don't believe you.

JACK: I'll prove it to you. Here comes a young lady now. (*A stunning brunette enters from stage left.*) Eh ... young lady!

BRUNETTE: Yes? (*She stops. Jack waves the vial under her nose.*) Oh, honey! (*She steps close to Jack, embraces him and starts rubbing her hand over his neck and chest.*) Where have you been? I've missed you so! I have to go home to mother now, but don't forget that we have a date behind the post office tonight at eight o'clock. (*She steps back from Jack and grinds her hips slowly.*) Tonight at eight o'clock, behind the post office. Don't forget! (*After a terrific bump, she prances out stage right. Luke is pop-eyed. He stares after the girl, then he stares at Jack. Finally he reaches out his hand eagerly.*)

LUKE: Oh boy! Oh brother! Let me borrow that thing. Let me have it! (*Jack gives it to him, just as the beautiful Redhead enters from left stage. As she passes the men, Luke waves it under her rear. She goes right on, but stops a few feet away to fix her stocking. Luke turns furiously on Jack.*) It don't work! (*Jack takes the vial and approaches the Redhead.*)

JACK: Aw, you don't know how to use it. Here, I'll show you. (*He waves the vial under the Redhead's nose and she at once throws her arms around him and begins to caress him lasciviously.*)

REDHEAD: Oh, honey! Where have you been? I've missed you so! I have to go home to mother now, but don't forget that we have a date behind the post office tonight at eight o'clock! (*She steps back from Jack and grinds her hips slowly.*) Tonight at eight o'clock, behind the post office. Don't forget! (*After a terrific bump, she prances out stage right. Luke comes to Jack.*)

LUKE: Looks to me like you're going to be awful busy behind the post office at eight o'clock.

JACK: (*Staring after the Redhead*) Aw, that's nothing. With this little old love philter, I've been busier. Much busier!

LUKE: Let me borrow it. I know how to use it now. Let me borrow it just for tonight.

JACK: All right. But I want it back tomorrow. I'll come right here to this same spot tomorrow morning and I want you to give it back to me.

LUKE: (*Muttering*) You won't be able to walk tomorrow morning. (*Out loud.*) I'll be right here. Give it to me.

JACK: All right. Here it is. Now, you know how to use it, don't you? You just wave it under the girl's nose, like this. (*He demonstrates with Luke, who weaves a little, rolls up his eyes.*)

LUKE: Ye … e … e … es! Ummmmm! That smells good.

JACK: All right. You take it now and good luck! (*He leaves at stage right.*)

LUKE: (*Looking toward stage left*) OK. Come on, you girls, I'll give you a little whiff of this. Oh boy! What a time I'm going to have! Just a little whiff like this (*He takes a whiff and reels slightly*) and you'll be mine, all mine! Just a little bitty whiff like this (*He takes another whiff and wobbles a little more*) and … and (*He takes another whiff.*) goodness gracious, but it smells good! (*He swishes his hips a little and takes another whiff.*) Oh boys! Gwacious! (*He takes another whiff and swishes about the stage a bit. A man enters from stage left and Luke swishes toward him, holding out his arm.*) Going my way, dearie?

(BLACKOUT)

Centerville was outraged!

Was this the great dream that had prompted Lula's parents to invest their savings in a college education for the girl? Was this being an "actress?" A brazen hussy, stripping naked on the stage! Centerville buzzed with the shock. Never had such a sensation struck the little town. Who would have thought such a thing of that little blonde Lang girl? Well! You never knew, did you, about these little innocent-looking ladies? What a thing she'd turned out to be! An "actress," Hah! Spending her parents' money, writing home how she had gotten a job playacting, getting everybody all het up. And now this. Well!

Of all the shocked people in Centerville, Tom Burke, the football player of Lula's early experience, now a young and successful insurance-man-about-town, was one of the most startled. He remembered Lula's shock at the experience they had had together and her refusal to have anything further to do with him. He could hardly believe that this was the same girl.

As bachelor president of a stag club, known as the Rams, he was subjected to a certain amount of ribald ribbing about Lula. Most of the young men in the organization had known Tom and Lula when they were in high school together and they knew how strongly Tom had felt about the girl. He tossed it off as best he could, but inside himself he was at a loss to understand his own feelings. He was not what one would call a bohemian, and although, as most men, he would be among the first to enjoy a good strip, he most certainly did not approve of women who did such a thing for a living. He would never have dreamed of marrying one, for instance, nor would he, had he already been married, ever have dreamed of bringing such a loose woman into contact with his wife. When he went and saw the girlie shows at the annual Legion Carnivals, he always managed to sneak away to them and to make every effort to avoid detection by his friends. In short, like any normal American male, he suffered badly from all the usual male urges, and indulged them with the usual secretiveness and covert shame.

It was a stunning blow to him that the small, blonde girl who had always occupied a high pedestal in his mind had fallen so suddenly and so definitely into the dust.

He went to see Lula's parents. They sat self-consciously on the porch, filling ten minutes with awkward overtures devoted to weather and crops and insurance.

Nobody said anything for a long while after that and the silence grew oppressive. Suddenly, in the dusk of the evening, Tom became aware that Mrs. Lang was crying. He made a small inadvertent movement toward the old lady and she knew that her weeping had been discovered. She lifted her head and tried to see the young man through her tears. "Oh, Tom," she cried, "what are we going to do? We just aren't the kind of people who can take this sort of thing lightly. It's been four days now since that awful column came out. We haven't written to Lula. We haven't done anything except sat here and watched all our old friends with their backs to us. We just don't know what to do."

"What do you suppose could have made her do such a thing, Mrs. Lang?"

"Oh, Lord, Tom, I don't know. I simply don't know! God knows what she learned up there at that college. God knows what kind of a girl they turned her into. Lula is not naturally this kind of girl."

Tom thought uncomfortably of a passionate abandoned night on Waterworks Hill a few years back, and he thought that he knew something about the potentialities of the Langs' daughter that the parents did not know. But passion did not necessarily mean that she had to become a stripper. "She must have had a reason," he said miserably.

The old man spoke up for the first time. "Reason!" he cried, "what is there of reason in a young, clean girl with a good background and an expensive education making a naked spectacle of herself and bringing complete disgrace on her parents and her home town?"

"Why don't you write her?"

Mrs. Lang sobbed aloud, "Write her? What can we write her? What can we write her besides beratings and scoldings? What have we to say to a girl we reared to become what she is?"

"You could tell her to stop."

"We could do that, all right. But she is fifteen hundred miles away and we can't go where she is. If she has turned into that kind of a girl, will a letter from her old parents make any difference to her?"

Tom was indignant. "Of course it will make a difference to her. Maybe she doesn't know what she is doing."

"She *must* know what she is doing. Every time I think of her I am sickened at the idea of what she is doing. Believe me, Tom, no woman could bring herself to practice such a profession without knowing what she was doing."

"Write her a letter, all the same, won't you, Mrs. Lang? Tell her to come home and then talk to her about it."

Out of the depths of his chair, the old man spoke bitterly. "Home? To make a spectacle of herself and of us? Maybe she can get a job with one of those carnivals that stop by here in the summer and then everybody could get a good look at her."

Mrs. Lang looked long at her husband. "Don't talk like that, Will. It doesn't make it any easier."

"I'm sorry," Mr. Lang said, "you're right. It doesn't make it any easier."

Lula got the letter on her eighth night as a featured stripper in the Brunswick Theatre.

A change had come over Lula … a change that Margot Diego had watched with growing interest. The frightened girl was gone and in her place was a shrewd, young show business woman. The change had been too fast. Margot could not believe it. There seemed to be a kind of defiance in it. Lula now went on stage boldly and unhesitantly. Her trepidation had lasted only two or three nights. After that, she held up her head and concentrated on her act. She had spent long hours every day, working it out, trying different types of costumes, familiarizing herself with the ancient art of the bump-and-grind. Although it probably had not as yet reached its highest peak of perfection, it was an artful, fantastically clever, planned version of her first night's torment. She still seemed to writhe with embarrassment, she still hesitated excruciatingly, she still wept and finally laughed hysterically. She still threw herself on the floor in the center of the stage at the climax of the strip. But everything was carefully worked out, plotted and arranged by now in such a manner that the men in the audience were carried breathlessly from excitation to excitation until at the end they were almost screaming with released tension. She was magnificent. Customers flocked to the Brunswick to see her and Margot.

And the money, the big money that she was getting. The very mention of such a sum had been enough to quell her fears of stripping.

Joe was in the process of frantic morning rehearsals to reshape the show to fit around the two contrasting women. He had set the big opening day a week into the future and he could hardly contain himself with anticipation. It was to be the greatest, most lavish display of burlesque to be exhibited in the United States since the theatres in New York had been closed. New Jersey was going to reverberate with the impact. He had sent out special invitations to all his old influential friends, to all the most important politicians, to all the nightclub columnists and critics. It was to be a gala occasion.

The poor chorus girls who had always gotten away with sloppily meandering through their routines suddenly found themselves drilled like Rockettes. The wardrobe mistress was spurred on to devising magnificent creations of body-displaying garments. A swishy, but tremendously capable dance director was imported from New York. He was a tough taskmaster. He was excellent. He wore tights and a beret. But he got results.

Early in the week, the older chorines eyed with suspicion an influx of fresh eighteen-year-olds who pranced about on the stage in bathing suits and shorts, and who disappeared one by one into Joe's office to display their wares. Their suspicions were not unfounded. At the end of the week only four of the younger members of the original chorus were still employed by the Brunswick, the rest were pounding the pavement looking for jobs again, their places taken by fresh young faces, fresh young bodies.

But the most amazing thing about it all was Lula. A sort of bitter defiance had taken hold of her. She who had always been gentle and softspoken and reticent, now snapped at people and made them feel that she was a star. She referred to her new profession with bitter anger and swept around the theatre like a prima donna.

It had taken her just exactly three days to move to a first-class apartment hotel. It had taken her four days to acquire a good sized wardrobe of expensive clothes. It had taken her five days to start drinking Scotch.

She lived alone, and after the shows were all over she fled the theatre, took a taxi through the tunnel and went alone to her hotel. Here she poured herself a liberal drink of Scotch, the taste of which she hated, put on her expensive nightgown and negligee and sat down to stare out of the window, out over the rooftops of the city.

She avoided Luke. She was always alone. And as she sat there staring out into the night, all the loathing for herself and her associates, all the disappointment, all the frustration and bitterness sat in her throat like sour bile.

"What can you do? What's your specialty? That's what the public buys!" She felt like leaning out the window and spitting hot venom on the public.

But there were times when alcohol could drown her disappointment ... or shopping for new additions to her fancy wardrobe, or entering an impressive nightclub where the headwaiter recognized her and seated her with honor.

Luke kept trying to corner her backstage. He pleaded with her. He tried to console her by explaining the expediency of intermediary steps in her career.

Her career! She laughed at him when he mentioned it. *This* was her career. *This* was what she had prepared herself in college for. *This* then was the end-all and the be-all of Lula Lang, actress aspirant.

She sent him packing with harsh words. When he begged her then, to quit something she hated so much, she replied in Hansel's words—"What's your specialty!" And sometimes she would laugh and cry at the same time, her loathing for herself and for her life so strong that she thought her heart would burst with it. And Luke would slink away like a whipped dog and she would either go to a nightclub by herself, repulsing all advances from eager swains, or home to her apartment to drink in solitude.

She did not answer the letter for two weeks. She did not know what to answer. Her name was still in all the columns of the night life. She knew only too well that it appeared again and again in her home town paper. It was too late for her to curse herself for not having changed her name on that first fateful night. It had never occurred to her at the time. She had been too scared to think of anything but to get it over with. Now it was too late. Too late, and she did not know what to do.

So she waited. Inside her was a crazy hesitancy which seemed to promise that if she just waited long enough, this would all go away and she would again be Lula Lang who lived in a room in the Village and had high hopes and magnificent dreams.

But she knew that she could not go back to that life deliberately. It would have to just simply happen. She could not get away from her fame and from the admiring accolades of the men she pleased. Hiding would do her no good. They would find her and force her to continue. She was trapped. She did not know how to answer her mother's letter.

The first letter had been a simple plea, for the sake of her mother and father to come home and explain Frank Powell's column.

It was when the second letter came that she realized that she could not wait any longer for the miracle that would make everything as it had been before she came in contact with Hansel

Schnitzler, with the Brunswick Theatre, with Margot Diego, and with Joe Pastelli. The second letter recounted how all her parents' friends were looking at them askance, how the boys in the pool-room laughed at her mother, how her parents' whole existence had crumbled, leaving burnt ashes and loneliness and fear, and complete lack of understanding as to what had happened to their little girl.

She decided to face the music. She sat by her window and took a deep draught of her Scotch and decided that somehow or other an even keel would have to be put under her existence again or she would go mad.

She went to Joe Pastelli.

He was reading clippings in his office, chewing his eternal cigarette, and there was a pleased smile on his face. She remained standing by the door. When he looked up and saw her there, he leaped to his feet, grinning as if he were demented, and motioned her to a chair by his desk.

"Lula! Come in. Come in." He picked up the pile of clippings. "Have you read these? We're wowing them. Here, read this one!" He thrust the clipping toward her, but she shook her head. "Aw, don't be modest! You're a sensation. It's John Terrence—he says you're the hottest thing since Helen of Troy. Think of that! Whoever the hell *she* was, she must have been something, if she was as good as you. I wonder where she stripped—I'll have to look it up. Maybe she's still in the business. I can put her in the show with you and Margot and there won't be nobody who can beat us! Here, read the darn thing." He thrust it at her again.

"Mr. Pastelli …" she started.

He interrupted her. "Joe. Joe, Lula. To you it's always Joe."

She continued. "… I want to talk to you."

"Sure, sure, honey. Any time. Just make yourself comfortable and spill it."

He was like a little boy petting and playing with his new puppy who had just won the first prize in the dog show. He ran about, his hands fluttering, waving the clippings, fussing over her. He turned her stomach.

Finally she spoke firmly. "Look, Mr. Pastelli, I want to quit."

He gaped at her open-mouthed. Then his face slowly dissolved into a stupid, staring grin. "Eh? … eh … hah? Oh … oh, I see! Oh, now, honey, I'm already milking myself. Don't do this to me."

"I don't want more money, Mr. Pastelli, I want to leave. I shouldn't have gotten myself into this in the first place. I have no business here. It's making me sick!"

He was all solicitude. "Honey-child, what's the matter?" He broke into revolting baby talk. "Has oo got a tummyache?"

She was disgusted. "Don't make a fool of yourself, Mr. Pastelli. There's nothing wrong with me that quitting won't cure. I'm not cut out for this and I simply can't stand it any more. So I am leaving."

She rose to go. Joe jumped to his feet and charged after her, grabbing her by the arm. "Now, wait a minute, Lula! For a second there I thought you wanted dough or that you were sick. What's the matter?"

"I *am* sick, in a way. Not physically. Not anything a doctor could cure. I am sick of myself. I am sick of this theatre and this show and what I'm doing in it. I came to New York to be an actress."

"Well, aren't you? Aren't you an actress?"

"I don't mean like that. I mean in plays."

"Ah …" his contempt was monumental, "they aren't here to stay. Plays are dead. What kind of dough do you think you could make, walking on as a maid or something? You're a star. You make tons of money. You can have everything you want. What the hell are you talking about?"

"I don't think you'd understand," she answered, her lips trembling. "I spent years preparing myself to make a name as an actress … not as a stripper … I was proud that I was going to be in an honorable profession, that I was going to be an ... an artist ..."

He interrupted her. "An artist! Why, you're the greatest piece of torso art I ever saw! What do you mean, an artist?"

"It's no use talking to you, Mr. Pastelli. I am miserable doing what I am. I want to get out."

Joe finally got mad. "Why, you lousy little mouse! Who took you out of the chorus? Who discovered you when you were a nobody? Who gave you your chance? Who made a star of you?" He waited impressively, but she did not answer. She simply looked at the floor. Finally he went on, "Joe Pastelli, that's who! I scooped you practically from the gutter, when you couldn't get anything to do, except prancing around in the chorus. Oh, don't look up with those injured eyes. I've talked to Hansel Schnitzler. He told me how you came to him like a whipped puppy. When I picked you up you had tried all the agents for plays and you hadn't gotten anywhere. You weren't nobody when I boosted you up to the top. Do you think you're going to walk out on me now? We got a contract, see?"

Lula sighed wearily. "All right," she said. "In that case I'll have to break my contract. I would rather spend the rest of my life paying you the money you'll sue me for than continue in your show."

Joe tried cajoling. "Look, honey," he purred. "You're the greatest thing in show business at this moment. You're valuable property. I just couldn't let you quit. Can't you see that? I spent a fortune on this show. It's only been running a little over a week. I haven't even started getting my investment back yet. Don't do this to me."

"I'm sorry, but if I don't quit, I won't be able to live with myself for the rest of my life."

"Honey, you won't have to live with yourself. I can name you any number of guys who'll be happy to keep you company."

Lula stood up. "I didn't mean to be funny." She started out the door, but again Joe intercepted her. "Please, honey. Please, every cent I've got in the world is staked on you."

"I wish I could help you, Mr. Pastelli. I can understand how you must feel, but there'll be other women and your money won't be lost, in the long run. Every cent you have in the world couldn't buy my life. Surely you can understand that."

"Understand? Understand? I don't understand nothing! I just understand that I'll sue the panties off you if you walk out on me now."

"I'm sorry you feel that way. In that case I'll just have to work extra hard in order to pay for your suit." Again she started out. This time Joe stopped her humbly. He was almost crying. "Look, Lula, honey, do something for me. Please! I'm begging you. Just go for a week's vacation, huh? Come back after a week. If you need rest, if you need to get something straightened out in your mind, go and straighten it out, but don't make this final. Please. I'm telling you, when you get away, you'll miss the old Brunswick. You'll miss us. You'll miss all the nice money when you're eating a bologna sandwich. Don't make this final. I can make good publicity hay of it, if I can say that the strain on your innocence has been so hard on you that you have had to go into seclusion for a little bit, but that as soon as you find your courage again you'll be back. You will force yourself to appear in public again. Do this for me, please, huh? Don't ruin my business like this."

Lula thought, what's the difference? I just won't come back. She said, "All right," and left the office. She went to her dressing room to pack. She walked right by Margot with hardly a nod of her head. She was through with this rotten business.

Margot had been studiously leaving her alone for three weeks now, and the two had been on fairly friendly terms. When the Latin stripper had found out what a tremendous impression the little blonde had made on her husband, she had decided to let matters rest for a while. At least to let them rest until Lula was ripe.

Now she looked after Lula and hurried up the fly-floor stairs to Joe's office. "What's with the virgin?" she asked as she came in the door.

"She is leaving," said Joe glumly.

"She is what?"

"Leaving! Quitting!" He stared angrily at Margot. "Why the hell did I ever let you get me into this mess?"

Margot smiled slowly and looked toward the door. "She'll be back," she said, "she'll be back."

Joe looked scornfully at her. "I wish I could be as sure of that as you seem to be."

Margot laughed and came to perch on his desk. "Don't let it get you. She's caught in the trap now. Once a stripper, always a stripper. You just wait."

The train clicked the miles off as Lula sat in her compartment feeling Centerville coming closer and closer. She stared at the passing landscape without seeing it. In her lap was a magazine, but she had not opened it.

She knew that her life had come to some sort of a climax. All she could do was hope that she would be able to cope with it. She had learned a lot during the last couple of months. She had grown up, and now the stars were out of her eyes. She realized with dismay that the stars were not out of Centerville's eyes— she could understand their shock and disappointment. It was her hope that when she got there she could explain something to her folks about growing up and taking life as it comes. That she could make them understand that youthful dreams and the final result are practically never the same thing. She now realized that her dream had been a dream of doing something she was good at on the stage ... not just acting, but satisfying an inner hunger in herself for fulfillment on the stage. That and ... yes, she could not deny it ... money! When she was a child, they had always had to scrape the bottom of the barrel in order to drum up enough money to let her go to the movies or get a new dress.

The night she had her big experience with Tom Burke, she was wearing a pair of sandals that had represented a sacrifice for her parents. When she went to school away from home, she had gone with the realization that every book she bought, every milkshake she drank constituted a major expenditure. She knew now that back of her mind for all these years had been the desire to make enough money to be able to laugh at the possibility of financial hardship. She knew that this idea had become a sort of obsession with her and that actually her dream had not been so much of *artistic* success in the theatre as of *financial* success. She had lulled her idealism to sleep with the idea that the two were synonymous, which in a way they were. But there were many ways of making money on the stage, and she happened to have fallen into one that she seemed particularly fitted for, and although she did not quite approve of its vulgarity, she could not give it up now.

She ran her hand over the silk that covered her leg. She was pleased with the rich sensuous feel of the material. She enjoyed the firm, rounded feeling of her thigh as she touched it. She was not as startled at herself as she had been three weeks ago, when she had lain on the floor of the Brunswick stage and realized that she was proud of her own body, that she was proud of the effect of that body on the men in the audience.

She remembered a psychology course she had taken in college which had mentioned something called "exhibitionism." The instructor had pointed out that there was a little bit of healthy exhibitionism in every woman. He had illustrated this by showing the students pictures of women's fashions. He had pointed out that for the most part women's clothes were designed to display the body. "The only reason women don't go naked in the first place," he had said, "is that most of them would be sorry spectacles that way." He had laughed then. "You see now, don't you, why there is such a tremendous market for foundation garments." She had been shocked at that. But she knew now that most men, in spite of their dirty little minds, saw only beauty in the naked body of a beautiful woman. She also realized that truly beautiful women were very rare, which is why a truly beautiful woman could make an exceptional living simply by displaying that beauty.

She realized that she knew a lot more about men and women and life than she did, such a short time ago. And she was no longer ashamed of having something worth displaying. She smiled as she thought of Luray Caverns and the Natural Bridge and Linville Caves. They were simply objects of nature being displayed for money. So was she. She was a natural object being displayed for money. Like the Grand Canyon. Like Grandfather Mountain.

What she had told Joe Pastelli had not been quite true, she knew now. She had not left the Brunswick because she was sick of displaying herself. She had left it because she had been frightened by the echoes in her parents' letters of a life that she had actually, without realizing it, left behind.

Now, as she sat in the train, she knew it. She had graduated from not knowing what she was doing, to knowing *exactly* what she was doing.

It was quite a revelation for little Lula Lang. When she had thought it through, she felt better. She no longer felt ashamed of herself. She felt satisfied that she had taken her particular place in the scheme of things and no one could blame her …

The train clanged into the station and she jumped off onto the platform. She had been unwise in her choice of costume for the return home. Had she returned in something simple, a small collegiate cotton frock of some kind, or some other unobtrusive costume, she might have got off to a better start. Unfortunately she had thought to please her mother by displaying her prosperity. But Centerville was a small town. It looked askance at sheerly stockinged legs and swirling silk, at platform shoes and overly high heels. All of these were the trademarks of sin in the large cities.

The small fur stole over shoulders did not help any, neither did the luxurious luggage, respectfully deposited at her feet by the porter.

Her mother simply stared at her.

Lula ran to her and enfolded her in a perfumed embrace. "Mother!" she cried, and instantly felt the older woman's obvious stiffening within her arms. She tried to kiss her face, but her mother turned away.

"Hello, Lula."

"Aren't you going to welcome me home?" Lula stepped back and regarded her mother curiously. There were tears of self-pity in Mrs. Lang's eyes.

"Why, I ... I hardly know what to say to you," her mother mumbled. "Let's go home," she continued as she became aware of the many eyes which were regarding them with curiosity from all around.

Lula covered up her confusion and sense of loss with a tinkling, gay little laugh. "All right!" She looked around her with bright eyes. "Is Tony still running the old cab? Let's see if we can find him and get him to take us home." As she looked around for the taxi driver, she saw several familiar faces in the crowd that had come down as usual to see the westbound express come in. She waved gaily at several of them and called "Hello!" in a cheery voice, but only one or two ventured as much as a timid response; the rest of them simply stared at her or turned away in embarrassment.

She was aghast at the reaction of her home town to her arrival. Meekly, she walked through the waiting room to the street outside and found Tony there, sitting comfortably in his cab. He had never made too much of trying to drum up trade from the people who got off at the station. His philosophy had always been that if people wanted a cab, they would come to him.

He smiled when he saw her and stepped out of the decrepit old rattletrap that served him as a place of business. "Well, Lula," he said, "how's the girl?"

Lula was tickled to death to find someone in her home town who appeared glad to see her. She shook old Tony's hand

and asked him to get her baggage from the station platform. He ambled off to comply with her instructions, saying over his shoulder as he went, "Some homecoming, huh?"

It was some homecoming, all right. Ten times worse than she had expected, but she had every intention of changing all that. If she could just make them understand!

In the cab on the way home, she tried unsuccessfully to approach her mother, to reach some ground of common understanding. She had had a pretty fair idea of the shock her new profession would be to her home town and to her folks, but she had not realized how much of an outcast she had made of herself.

Then the cab drew up at the curb in front of her home, and leaving Tony to worry about the luggage, she jumped out and dashed across the narrow lawn to where her father was sitting on the porch. She threw herself to her knees in front of him and flung her arms about him.

"Daddy!" she cried.

"Hello, Lula." He sat stiffly with her arms around him.

She released him slowly and pulled back and looked intently at him with wide eyes. Fear was beginning to churn within her. This was worse than she had expected. Much worse! She was still not too far from being the little girl not to be afraid of her parents.

She stood up slowly, on weak knees. Fumbling in her purse, she paid off the sadly smiling Tony.

After he had gone, Lula and her parents remained on the porch, looking at each other. All three were lost. Somehow, what was burning in them could not be put into words.

Finally Will said, "Let's go inside. We're making a spectacle of ourselves out here on the porch. Give me a hand, Anne."

Mrs. Lang helped him to his feet, and leaning on her shoulder, he humped slowly through the front door into the house. They left Lula standing there amidst her baggage, completely at a loss as to what to do.

She followed them in, her knees shaking under her. They were both sitting in the half-darkened parlor, neither saying anything.

Lula stopped by the door. "Look," she began, then faltered and just stood there, unable to go on. The two old folks looked at her with unseeing eyes.

"Look at her," said her father at last. "Look at her standing there in that floozy dress."

Lula looked down at her dress in bewilderment. It was a beautiful dress and she had put it on with pride this morning on the train. Now suddenly it was sordid and slinky and lacked only the scarlet satin to be the dress of a streetwalker. Her hands went involuntarily in front of her, as if to hide the garment which so offended her father.

"I'd have thought you'd have come with a carnival," he muttered miserably, "so as you'd have had a chance to display your wares. Your mother tells me that the boys down at the poolroom can hardly wait."

Lula stared at her father, completely shocked. Never in all her life had she heard him speak so bitterly. Never had she known him to be crude or vulgar.

"Daddy," she whispered, hanging her head so that she would not have to look at him. "Mother ... please, you don't understand ..."

"We understand well enough," said her father.

"No ... please, please listen to me. What happened was out of my control. It just happened. I tried to get a job. I tried and tried, but the money was giving out. I just couldn't come home. Can't you understand that?"

Her parents said nothing and she went on desperately. She *had* to make them understand somehow. "I went to all the agents, all the men who could give me jobs. Don't you see? I had such big dreams." And almost accusingly, she added, "We *all* had such big dreams. Don't you remember? All the things I was going to do? Everybody expected so much of me. I just couldn't come home without having gotten anywhere."

Her mother twisted her mouth bitterly. "Do you call this getting somewhere?"

"Mother, please! Please listen to me and try to understand. You were always writing to me, telling me about your big hopes for me and how much money you had spent on getting me ready for it and how the town thought I would be a big thing some day and how I was going to put Centerville on the map. Don't you see that I couldn't come home?"

"All we can see is what you made of yourself, girl," said her father.

"No, no. When I couldn't get a job, I went to an agent who hires chorus girls for these theatres. He got me a job. It was harmless. I just danced in a chorus. Lots of girls dance in choruses for a start! There was nothing wrong with it. Then the producer wanted me to … to … do what I am doing now and I said no. I said *no*, mother! Doesn't that mean anything to you? I wouldn't do it. I hated him for telling me to and I walked out. I quit. I was going to come home."

"Why didn't you? Why didn't you spare us this disgrace?"

"When I was walking out of the theatre, I got your letter about you and father needing money. I just couldn't come home then. I just *had* to make some money. A lot of money, so I could pay you back!" She fumbled in her purse. "Look. Look, what I brought you! Here's a thousand dollars. A thousand dollars, mother! That's a lot of money. And there'll be a lot more. You'll never know want again as long as you live. I can buy you anything you want. But please, please don't hate me any more. It was the only thing I could do."

She held the money out toward her parents, but neither made a single gesture toward taking it. Finally she pulled her outstretched hand back and stood there against the wall, huddled like a little hurt animal, whimpering a little now and then.

"Take your dirty money," said her father, "and you know what you can do with it!" He shuddered at his own vulgarity. "Go out to the fairgrounds and strip naked for the boys. That's where you belong!"

"I did it for you. For *you!*"

Her father looked her over scornfully. "I don't suppose you enjoyed it?"

"That doesn't have anything to do with it. I hated it that first time. I have never been so ashamed in my life. I wanted to crawl into a hole."

"Why didn't you?" her mother retorted. "We'd all have been better off. And what about the second time and the third? I suppose you hated them, too?"

"No, mother," Lula was honest, "I didn't. But mother, that is just something I discovered about myself. I can't help it. I didn't put it there."

"Are you trying to say that this is our fault?" her father wanted to know.

"No, daddy. It is nobody's fault. It just happened, like I told you."

"Well, it can just unhappen again. No daughter of mine is going to go around making an exhibit of her own naked body. We don't have a friend left in Centerville."

"They will get over it."

"Over it? Get over that one of their neighbors' daughters is no better than a prostitute?"

"Daddy, daddy. Don't say things like that to me."

"But it's true, isn't it? It's true, every word of it! What's the difference between you and a girl in a house?"

Lula's mother was crying. "Oh, I'm so ashamed! I'm so ashamed! How could you do this to us? Standing there on the train platform this morning, feeling everybody's eyes on me. I have never been so ashamed in all my life!"

Then Lula knew that she would never be able to explain it to her parents. That they would never understand each other again, if indeed they had *ever* understood each other. She was still holding the thousand dollars in her hand. She dropped it on the floor and asked in a low voice, "What if I quit? What would I do? Could I come back here and start again?"

Her mother answered for her. "Not here," she muttered, "not here." And Lula realized that she was not thinking of her daughter's life, but of her own.

"I have quit, mother," she said quietly, finally gaining some measure of control over herself. "I have quit. When I came here, I told the producer that I would never do it again."

Her father sounded weary. "It isn't what you won't do, girl," he said, "it is what you *have* done. Everybody here knows you for what you are."

"But what am I to do? How am I to right this wrong I have done to you?"

"I don't know," sighed her father. "Get out of town again, maybe. Get far away and maybe your mother and I can live it down." Her mother said nothing. She only huddled in her chair, her face hidden in her hands.

Lula looked from one to the other. At last, she turned and opened the door. "Goodbye," she whispered, "goodbye." She stumbled out on the porch, picked up her suitcases, and went blindly down the stairs. When she had reached the center of the lawn, her mother appeared on the porch.

"Here," the woman cried, "take this with you; we don't want it!"

She threw the thousand dollars after Lula. It landed at her feet and she put down one suitcase and bent mechanically to pick it up. Balling the money in her fist, she picked up the suitcase again and went out into the street without looking back ...

In her room in Centerville's only hotel she threw herself down on the bed and cried herself to sleep. She stayed like that for four hours, and then late in the afternoon, she bathed and dressed herself with care. There was no train back east until the next day, but she refused to stay in her room like a nun doing penance. She went downstairs and into the little bar in the old hotel. It was one of those saloons which in the middle thirties had been turned into a newfangled "cocktail lounge." It was a small room with soft, indirect light over the bottles behind the counter and semicircular booths with imitation leather seats. She ordered a Scotch and soda and settled down to drinking the amber fluid. The bartender was old-fashioned. He must have known all about Lula, as did everyone in town, but he never let on. He ignored her and she was grateful for it.

She had been sitting there for almost an hour and had consumed four drinks when a large shadow loomed over her. She looked up into the blue eyes of Tom Burke.

She had not seen Tom since her last vacation from college, but she had certainly not forgotten him. She knew him at once and lowered her eyes.

"Hello, Lula," he said quietly. "May I sit down?"

She nodded toward the seat opposite her and he slid in under the table. He was silent for a long time and she did not look at him. Finally, she could stand the silence no longer and looked up to find him smiling gently at her.

"Had a tough time today, didn't you?" he said.

She nodded dumbly.

"Don't let them get you down."

She said sarcastically, "Can you afford to be seen sitting with me?"

He said, "Don't." And there was a pleading tone in his voice that made her look up in surprise. She suddenly realized that during all these years, Tom had not forgotten her. She was warmed by the knowledge. She was comforted and she found herself smiling at him.

He asked no questions, he said very little. He ordered more drinks and they drank them in silence. Finally, he said, "Tell me about it, Lula."

She had had too much to drink by then and her emotional heartstrings had been stretched beyond the point of endurance. She said bitterly, "Why do you want to know? Do you want to join the boys in the carnival tent?"

She was surprised when he laughed at that. It was not what you would call a nice laugh. "I'm interested," he said, "I'm interested beyond the point of the poor little hicks who have never known you as I have known you."

"Do you really remember, Tom?"

"I have never forgotten. Why couldn't you just have given that passion to me and not cast it before swine? I begged you so."

"I ... I ..."

"I know. You wanted more than that."

"Please don't gloat, Tom."

"I'm not gloating. God knows I am not."

The front door of the bar swung open and a group of four young men came in. They were all boys that Lula had gone to school with. They recognized her at once.

"Look who's here! Lula! How're you doin', baby?" They laughed and crowded around the table, squeezing into the narrow seats, one of them rubbing up close against her. She tried to move away, but was wedged in.

"Have we been wanting you to come back home, girl! How's about showing us a sample of your wares?"

"Please," she said helplessly, "please, don't."

But they went on, coarsely enjoying the situation. "How's about doing a job for us tonight? Mack here has always needed a floor show. Come on, Lula, let's see what you can do!"

The boy next to her let his hand drop on her thigh. She tried desperately to dislodge it, but he hung on, his fingers digging into the flesh.

Suddenly Tom stood up. "Which one of you boys wants to go out with me first?" he asked menacingly.

They looked at him, aghast. "Tommy! Tommy, don't be a piker! Do you want her all to yourself? How often does Centerville produce a national monument like her?" They laughed and Tom grabbed the nearest one by the scruff of the neck. He pulled the boy to his feet.

"Ernie. You want to be first? Or do I take you all at once? Now, beat it!"

The four boys got reluctantly to their feet. They moved toward the bar.

"Aw, lay off, you musclebound goon," said Ernie sheepishly. He stepped close to the bar. "Mack, bourbon-on-the-rocks here."

But Tom was not through yet. "Out!" he said. "I said out! Outside! Beat it, you yellow little rats!"

The boys slunk out of the lounge.

"I'm sorry, Lula," Tom said. "They don't know any better."

"It doesn't matter. I should get used to it. I'm a sensation, aren't I?"

"Well yes," he smiled, "you are, sort of."

"It isn't every day one of the girls they went to high school with takes up the profession I have taken up."

"Lula, don't scourge yourself, please."

"I had a rotten morning today," she said.

"I know. I knew you would have when I heard you were coming back."

"Would you like to hear about it?"

"No. No, thanks. Look, let's just eat. Let's forget about those fools and eat and have a good time and reminisce."

"Reminisce!" She laughed bitterly. "About what? Waterworks Hill?"

"I loved you, Lula! Can that brief episode still stick in your mind like this? After the things you've done? The things you've seen?"

"What have I seen? I do something for a living that nobody approves of—does that mean that I have led a dissolute life?"

"No, I didn't mean that."

"What did you mean?"

"Hell, I don't know. Let's eat."

They had steak for dinner. Steak and French fried potatoes. It was good, and little by little Lula loosened up with Tom Burke. She told him about college and Greenwich Village and Hansel Schnitzler and Margot and Joe Pastelli. She was enjoying herself and the three more Scotches she had with dinner didn't interfere with her fun.

Tom too was getting drunk. As he sat at the table opposite her, his body commenced to weave to and fro. He smiled at her in an asinine fashion and she took a good hold on the edge of the table with both hands.

She clung there with all her might. "The hell with the folks. The hell with all of them. I'm from the big city now. I don't care what they say!"

Tom applauded her enthusiastically. "Atta-girl! You tell 'em!"

It was maudlin and ugly and vulgar, but they were both at peace with the world. After a while, Lula said blearily, "You want to see me dance?"

Tom reared back in the booth. "I have a meetin'," he muttered.

"What kind of a meetin'?"

"The Rams Club."

"Wha's that?"

"Stag club. Bunch o' the boys."

"Tonight?"

"Night. Gotta go." He tried to get to his feet.

"You're drunk."

"Ain't either." He giggled like a fool.

Then the devil caught her. All the defiance came up in her and it felt as if a hot wave had passed behind her eyes. She threw back her head and laughed. This would show them! "What d'you do at the meetin's?"

"Drink. Drink and shoot the bull and play poker."

"No entertainment?"

"Sometimes."

"What?"

"Aw, you know … at carnival time … it's a stag club after all … should have some entertainment now an' again."

"How'd you like some entertainment tonight?"

He stared at her, his already bleary eyes watering a little with the effort. "What d'you mean?"

"Me. I'll come up and dance for the boys."

"Lula! You're off your trolley. What're you talking about? This is Centerville!"

"That's what I mean. That'd show 'em."

"Aw no, Lula. You'd ruin yourself for good and all."

"Aren't I ruined now?"

"No, I mean really! You'd never be able to set foot in this town again. Your folks would kill you, too."

"They're killing me now. They threw me out."

Tom looked at her for a long time. "All right," he said. "If you want to, why not?"

She laughed again. "Let's have another drink and then we'll go give the boys a thrill."

She reached for her glass, but tipped it over so the ice and the contents spilled out on the table. A drunken giggle parted her lips.

The Rams Club held its weekly meetings in the big room above an old store, now empty, situated behind the hotel, across the alley. The hall had originally been a storeroom belonging to one of the members of the club, but when the organization came into being two years previously, he had donated the space and they had all pitched in to move the innumerable boxes and crates of haberdashery downstairs into the old store. They had decorated the room with cheap paper streamers and set up card tables here and there for the purpose of poker playing. At one end of the room was a bar which was at all times kept well-stocked. Here they took business prospects to ply them with a little encouragement. Here, now and then, they threw a dance which generally turned into a drunken brawl. Here they spent a lot of their free time, repairing their fishing tackle in the company of other fishermen, cleaning their guns while they discussed the season with other hunters. They were all bachelors and the club meant a sort of home to them where they could always find congenial company.

Every Thursday night they had a "meeting." This consisted simply of a short statement of the club's finances and a long session of poker and talk. A lot of the talk was about women. Most of them were bored with Centerville and the club served as an escape. A man could shed his inhibitions and his social limitations to a certain extent. He could feel like a hell of a fellow, even though his days were spent cutting hair or selling shirts on Centerville's one and only business street.

There wasn't much to do for fun in Centerville. There were no nightclubs. There was only one movie house, the manager of which seemed to have a predilection for Westerns, all of which had the same plot. There were few eligible girls.

Most of the Rams agreed that the town was dead.

The only real excitement they had was in the fall when the carnivals came to town, sometimes two or three of them over a period of a couple of months. Then the president would be delegated to contact the girls in the girlie shows to offer them a good round sum of money to come and give a little private performance. Most of the time they came, and then the Rams had a big time.

On this particular Thursday the young men were resigned to discussing the shortcomings of Centerville, to play poker, and to get polluted. There seemed to be nothing else to do.

They were therefore delighted when Tom Burke turned up with Lula Lang and announced that when the proper moment arrived and the requisite amount of fuel consumed, she would favor them with a sample of her particular type of entertainment. Most of the men knew Lula and had known her for years. They knew her folks and were among the ones who had either turned their backs on the old people or scorned and mocked them since Lula had become famous ... or was "notorious" the word?

Now, they welcomed Lula enthusiastically. The place was hers. What could they do to help?

Well, they could give her a drink first of all. They did, and it was virtually undiluted.

Lula looked about her at the flushed eager faces. She had never been in such a situation before, and the feeling was not unpleasant. She was the lone object of the admiration of twenty-two young men and this knowledge, aided by the liquid in her glass, went to her head. She sat on the bar, her legs dangling, the center of a tight group of males all asking her questions about her work, all wanting to know about New York and New Jersey and burlesque. None of these men had ever paid too much attention to her when she was in high school. She had been quiet and unassuming and most of them had regarded her as being a little mousy. Now things were different. She was anything but mousy and the men were delighted with her and with themselves for being the possessors of such a catch.

The party progressed and the room got hotter and hotter with pent-up cigarette smoke and whiskey fumes and the heated bodies of many drinking men. A few poker games had been started by the more sophisticated, and Lula circulated among the tables, always with Tom by her side. She was getting drunker by the minute, her misery driving her on to greater heights in playing the big city burlesque queen visiting the little town.

Their eyes followed her wherever she went and their minds were hot with her. Liquid refreshments were flowing freely and little by little the men lost control over themselves. They began to pull her into corners and make lewd suggestions. They began to urge her to do her dance. They could not wait much longer.

Suddenly, Tom caught her by the arm and dragged her toward the door. She tried to resist, her drink splashing on the floor from the glass in her hand. But she was no match for the big ex-football player. No one seemed to notice them at the moment and he managed to get her beyond the screen which marked off a sort of front hall in the room. Here he stopped pulling at her, but kept a good hold of her arm.

"Look, Lula," he said. "Let's get out of here. I'm sorry we ever started it."

Lula weaved drunkenly. "Whassa matter with *you?*"

"Lula," he pleaded, "come on. This is no place for you."

"It's wha' I do for living," she muttered.

"Not this. Not like this! Please, Lula. Let's forget it. I just can't stand by and see this happen."

"Leggo o' me!" She cried and tugged at his hand. "It's my life! All those ... all those ..." she waved her hand vaguely, "all those so-an'-sos out there. Thissis wha' they wanna see. Well, we'll show 'em!" She lurched. "Callin' me names. I'll show 'em!"

She gave him a violent push which flung him back against the screen. The screen crashed to the floor and they stood revealed. The other men in the room laughed and roared and applauded as they shouted lewd suggestions to Tom as to how to deal with a wildcat. While he stood rooted to the spot, Lula stumbled into the center of the floor. She flung up her arms.

"All right, boys, put on your glasses, 'cause here we go!" She threw the glass with the remainder of her drink against the far wall and it crashed and splattered to the floor. "Who's goin' to play for me?"

One of the men rushed to the old battered piano that stood crammed in a corner, and struck a wild chord.

"No, no, no! You haven't got the idea. Soft an' sweet. Soft an' sweet."

Tom leaped over the screen, running toward her. Two of the men grabbed his arms from behind and held him as if in a vise.

The man at the piano tickled soft chords from the keyboard. Lula looked around her defiantly.

"It's all yours, boys," she muttered and then she began to move. She was not wearing anything that could be remotely construed as a stripper's costume, but she did not seem to care. With the beginning of the music she had stopped weaving and lurching and now appeared infinitely sure of her footing. The light from the naked bulbs glared down on her gleaming blonde hair.

As she walked slowly toward the right, she reached for the zipper at her side and jerked it down.

Gone was the innocent virgin! Gone was the cringing bride! There was only Jezebel, blazing with sex, abandoned, wanton …

With unbelievable gracefulness she pulled the dress off over her head and stood in her slip, her high heels planted firmly on the floor. She swayed a little and shook her head.

There was the silence of death in the room. The men were not stirring. They were staring. Staring.

Slowly and deliberately Lula walked to the edge of the floor. She stopped by one of the tables where the men were sitting motionless. She put her hand in the hair of one of them and rumpled it. Her hips were grinding slowly. Gently and slowly in small, promising motions.

Suddenly she jerked away from the man just as he was reaching an avid arm out for her. She backed to the center of the floor, and throwing her head back with a wild laugh, she gripped the front of her slip and tore it straight down. She threw it off her shoulders.

Her stockings were rolled at the middle of her thighs. Other than these and her shoes, she was wearing nothing but brassiere and panties of the most transparent nylon.

The men gasped and leaned tensely forward.

She was still laughing as she strode calmly around the floor to the soft chords from the piano. When she came back to the middle, she suddenly dropped to her heels and threw her arms behind her on the floor. Her hips ground madly for a moment, then she stood up again and reached behind her. The brassiere came off and her small breasts quivered in the light.

For a second she stood there, then she stooped to retrieve her gown.

"More! More! All the way!" A dozen hands reached out toward her, but she pulled back from them, smiling.

Tom struggled furiously against the men holding him. With a cry, he managed to break away from their restraining hands. He hurtled toward Lula. "You heard them!" he sobbed. "All the way!" He laughed hysterically as Lula stood her ground, a vacant, drunken smile on her face. Suddenly one of his hands shot forward, grasped the top elastic of her panties and ripped the tiny garment from her hips.

She stood naked and the men howled their approval. They thumped Tom on the back.

"What a dish!"

"Look what we've been missing!"

"And this was right here under our noses for years!"

"Boy, what the big city will do for a gal!"

Tom stood petrified for a long time, staring at the naked girl. She stared back at him, a hurt look in her eyes.

"Let's get outta here," he muttered after a long, painful moment.

Lula came peacefully. On the way across the floor, she stooped and retrieved her undergarments, crumpling them into an unobtrusive bundle. She went docilely, stumbling a little, giggling a little, her head lolling loosely as he helped her slip the dress over it.

At the door, she stopped. She turned and looked them over. "So long, boys," she said. "Don't forget to tell your mothers that Lula Lang gave her all for you. That'll set 'em on their ears."

In the deserted hotel, Tom guided her upstairs to her room and closed the door behind them. He reached for the bottom hem of her dress and pulled it upward over her head. He feasted his eyes and then pressed her backward until the back of her knees touched the edge of the bed.

"Don't," she muttered. "Don't, please. I've never done it. Please don't."

Then she fell back on top of the cheap hotel bedspread.

She cried out once. Then she whimpered as the world spun on its horizon and she clung to the warm male above her.

Later she lay on the bed, her small body twisting and tossing. There was no rest for her. It was as if she had just begun and had never finished what had been started. She closed her eyes. Whimpered …

Tom stood looking down at her, his mind a whirlpool of conflicting emotions. He could not count the years he had wanted this to happen, and now that it had happened, it had been all wrong. He did not know whether he hated her or loved her, whether he hated himself or approved of what he had done. He stood indecisive for a long time, then turned and left the room quietly.

Outside the door he stopped abruptly.

Seven men were sitting in a line against the wall, passing a bottle among them. They looked up expectantly and smiled lewdly. They stood up and crowded around him.

"What's she like?"

"You dirty swine," said Tom to his friends. To the barber, to the hardware merchant, to the salesman. "You dirty swine." He leaned weakly against the wall.

"Don't be a piker," they said, repeating what the boys in the bar had said earlier that evening, "do you wanna keep her all to yourself?"

Lula Lang was public property now. She was engaged in a profession that promised, and therefore men expected the promise to be fulfilled.

Tom looked from one to the other, but the faces he had known for years were not the same. There was something animal in them, something abandoned, something that he had never seen before and hoped never to see again. It had come to the surface tonight.

He knew that at least four of the seven would be in church the following Sunday. They would dismiss this unexpected escapade as being the fault of a little provocative tart of a girl. They would make their peace with themselves as they carelessly wiped away their guilt with a cliché about loose women.

He thought of the writhing body he had left on the bed.

A dreadful wave of despair and hopelessness poured through him. He did not even attempt to stop them. He buried his face in his hands and lurched away from the wall. Drunkenly weeping, he staggered down the hall to the carpeted stairs.

The barber went in first …

CHAPTER SIX

The city went right on with whatever it was doing. The great, sprawling city. The seething conglomeration of salesmen and stenographers, of millionaires and paupers. The subway went on roaring. The tunnels kept swallowing at one end and excreting at the other, spewing forth steady streams of humanity, smugly enclosed in their fuming forms of transportation, experiencing a momentary thrill at traversing the bowels of the earth under the river. Some of the cars went to suburban homes where they were greeted with the shrill cries of happy children; some went to the far-flung golf courses where cheeriness and synthetic happiness were consumed in large doses at the nineteenth hole; some went to narrow little out-of-the-way alleys, where their occupants got out furtively and rapped prearranged signals on closed doors. Some went to the Brunswick Theatre.

The Brunswick Theatre went right on with whatever it was doing.

No one knew about Lula. No one seemed to care. Even Luke, whose eyes had deepened in melancholy, appeared indifferent to her fate. He did not know. The theatre did not know. The city did not know.

The Brunswick did not stop functioning.

("In-One" in front of act curtain, displaying a large painted library wall covered with books. A large painted window showing a formal garden. A screen at stage-left, separating the

left end of the stage from the right, so that the audience can see both ends, but the actors on the stage cannot see who is on the other side of the screen. Enter Luke and Little Jack. Jack is carrying a violin. Luke is trailing behind him. He is very upset.)

LUKE: Now, look here, Little Jack, I just don't know what I'm going to do. I want to marry this girl and her father says that he will never let her marry anyone who is not a great musician. What'll I do?

JACK: (*With thick accent*) Issa goot you come to me, mine poy! I help. All you do is play the violin for papa and you're in!

LUKE: What're you talking about, violin? I can't play the violin.

JACK: Here, then, I show you. (*He displays the violin.*) Now looky here. This issa violin. Is fine instrument. Is very delicate. Is make *fine* music.

LUKE: OK. OK. I seen a violin before.

JACK: And you know something about, eh? You know what makesa music? Yes? No?

LUKE: No.

JACK: I explain. (*He holds up violin again.*) You see, here is a box? Yes?

LUKE: Yes.

JACK: Goot. We are agreed. Now look here. (*He holds up the bow.*) This ... (*He runs his finger along the hair on the bow.*) ... this we calla the horse's tail. Yes?

LUKE: Yes? So what?

JACK: So is simple. (*He runs his hands over the strings of the violin.*) Thissa we call the cats'es guts. Yes? No?

LUKE: All right, all right, get to the point.

JACK: (*Sticking a finger into one of the two vents in the violin*) Thissa is the greatest invention of all. Thissa we call the esse-hole. See?

LUKE: (*After snicker from audience has died down*) Look, I haven't got time for this nonsense.

JACK: Issa not nonsense. Issa music. Now, then. (*With great air of authority.*) To maka the music, we taka the horse's tail and runna it over the cats'es guts, see?

LUKE: Yes, yes, I see.

JACK: (*Triumphantly*) And the music, she is coming outta the esse-hole!

LUKE: (*After roar has died down in the house*) So how is that going to help me?

JACK: (*Sadly*) You canna play this fine insterument?

LUKE: No, I canna play this fine insterument.

JACK: Then I help you. I play it for you.

LUKE: But how?

JACK: (*Looks around*) Ah! Here is fine screen. I hide behind it. You get violin, and when you say, "All right," I play. See? Yes? No?

LUKE: (*Laughing*) I see! But what if we are discovered?

JACK: We no get discovered. When you say, "All right," and play, I play. Is simple.

LUKE: Fine, fine, get behind the screen. (*He rushes offstage while Jack goes to sit behind the screen in full view of the audience. Luke returns immediately with another violin. He goes to the other side of the screen from Jack, fondling the instrument lovingly. The Gorgeous Redhead enters. It is Little Jack's wife, Pee Wee again. She meets Luke at stage right. She cannot see Jack from where she is.*)

REDHEAD: Oh, Luke, what shall we do? Father won't let me marry anyone who is not a musician, and you are not one, and I can't live without you. (*She flutters her false eyelashes monstrously.*)

LUKE: Who says I am not a musician? Look, I brought my violin.

REDHEAD: Why, Luke, I never knew you could play a violin.

LUKE: (*Out of the corner of his mouth to the audience*) Neither did I. (*To the Redhead.*) Of course, I can play a violin. You want to hear me?

REDHEAD: Oh, yes, Luke, play something for me.

(*Luke puts the violin clumsily to his chin. He has some trouble getting his fingers arranged on the strings and tries to work with the bow upside down first, but eventually he gets in position. He strikes a Yehudi Menuhin stance and draws the bow across the strings. Not a sound comes forth. He smiles weakly at the Redhead. Jack, behind the screen is dozing peacefully in his chair. Luke tries to start playing again, but not a sound comes forth from the sleeping Jack. Luke is frantic.*)

LUKE: (*Suddenly remembering*) Ask me again to play.

REDHEAD: Oh, Luke, darling, play something for me on the violin.

LUKE: All right. (*He again draws the bow over the strings, but Jack is asleep. He speaks loudly.*) All right! (*Jack remains snoozing comfortably. Luke screams.*) ALL RIGHT! (*Jack wakes up with a start and begins furiously to play "Keep the Home Fires Burning." He almost manages to catch Luke off base, but by rushing furiously with the bow, Luke appears to catch up and seems to play beautifully through the selection. At the end of the piece, he lowers the violin, but Jack is not through yet. He plays, with gusto, "Shave-and-a-haicut-two-bits." Luke almost breaks his jaw getting the violin up in time to appear to be the one playing it. Jack drops back into his doze again and Luke breathes a sigh of relief.*)

REDHEAD: (*Admiringly*) Oh, Luke, you are wonderful. Wait till I tell Papa. (*She calls offstage.*) Papa! Come here and hear Luke play the violin.

(*Papa comes in from stage-right. An old straight-man, he has the appearance and the sonorous tones of a broken down Shakespearean actor.*)

PAPA: Yes, yes, my dear daughter, here I am. What do you want? (*He spies Luke.*) Get out of here, you little rat. You have no business courting my darling daughter. My father was a musician, my grandfather before him, and so on ad infinitum. I will never let my little Geraldine marry anyone but a great musician.

REDHEAD: But Luke *is* a musician. He *is* great. Wait till you hear him play the violin!

PAPA: Play the violin? Why, that is wonderful! If he can play it to my satisfaction, I will be glad to let him marry you. (*To Luke.*) Go ahead and play it, son.

LUKE: All right. (*He lifts the bow to his chin and starts to draw the violin across it.*)

PAPA: What are you doing?

LUKE: I'm going to play the violin.

PAPA: With the instrument on the bow?

LUKE: (*Quickly reversing the position*) Oh ... (*He laughs weakly.*) That's just how we used to do it in the mountains of Tennessee.

PAPA: Oh well, play the violin now. (*As Luke raises his violin.*) Is that a Stradivarius?

LUKE: A what?

PAPA: A Stradivarius.

LUKE: (*Frantically, as he tries to adjust his trousers*) Oh, gosh, is that damn thing unzipped again?

PAPA: No, no. I mean is that an expensive violin?

LUKE: Oh, yes. Very expensive. One forty-nine in Gimbel's basement.

PAPA: Well, play it, play it!

LUKE: All right! (*He raises the violin again. No sound comes from behind the screen where Jack is snoozing peacefully.*) ALL RIGHT, GODDAMMIT! (*Jack leaps into action, playing "Keep the Home Fires Burning" with great gusto. This time Luke is cagey, he keeps the violin at his chin after the piece is over and sure enough here comes "Shave-and-a-haircut-two-bits." Luke has triumphed and he doesn't mind showing it.*)

PAPA: (*Impressed*) Very beautiful, very beautiful! Especially the arpeggio in the last movement. (*Luke makes an involuntary movement toward his fly. It is zipped.*) It was beautiful. Do it again.

LUKE: All right. (*This time Jack is there with his violin before Luke even gets a chance to get his instrument up to his chin. He ends up having to play it in his lap like a trick mountain fiddler. But it works. At the end of the piece, he looks up triumphantly.*) Look, no hands, how's that? (*But he has forgotten the "Shave-and-a-haircut" and is caught again. He never makes that one and Papa looks puzzled.*)

PAPA: How's that? You play without playing?

JACK: Oh, this little violin is all right. (*Jack starts furiously again and poor Luke just manages to get his violin up in time.*)

PAPA: This is fine. I like you. You can marry my daughter. (*Luke and the Redhead fling themselves in each other's arms.*) Please, play it for me once again. I love music.

LUKE: (*Bringing the instrument to his chin. He is going to really slay Papa*) All right. (*He draws the bow across the instrument while the Redhead looks on adoringly. No sound. He draws the bow across again. No sound.*) All right, I said! (*No sound.*)

PAPA: Yes, you said all right. Please, play it again. (*He leans back, his head raised, his eyes closed.*)

LUKE: (*Frantically*) ALL RIGHT! (*Jack leaps into action behind the screen, but no sound comes from his violin. He scrapes the bow madly acress the strings, but no sound comes. Luke yowls.*) ALL RIGHT! (*Jack is desperate. He plucks the strings, no sound comes. He digs his fingers into the vents in the violin, trying to clear them. It does not help. Luke screams.*) ALL RIGHT! (*Papa looks at him in amazement. The Redhead moves closer to him, solicitously, as he frantically saws back and forth with the bow on the violin. His back is to the screen. Jack emerges from his hideout, holding his violin out apologetically.*)

JACK: Please, peoples, a little castor oils. The esse-hole, she is stopped up!
(BLACKOUT)

Lula lay all that night on the mess of crumpled sheets in a daze. Once, at four in the morning, while the window was still a black, yawning hole in the wall and the naked light bulb in the ceiling, which had cast its garish light on what had happened to her earlier was still glaring, she got up slowly and painfully, her loins screaming in agony. For a long time she stood by the bed, nausea churning in her stomach, and looked at the stains of blood where they had formed dark splotches in the center of the wrinkled, sweat-soaked sheets. She stumbled to the bathroom and dug her razor out of the little overnight bag which had been put there. She took the blade out meticulously, careful not to cut herself. Then, sitting on the edge of the bathtub, she held the sharp edge against her wrist for a long time.

But she did not have either the courage or the will to slit the artery.

After a while she replaced the blade in the razor, put it mechanically back in the bag again, and went back to bed. She tried to straighten the sheets out a little, but her back hurt her so, and she was so indifferent to her surroundings that she ended up by simply falling forward on her face and remaining in that position.

She did not weep. She felt virtually nothing, except the physical pain. It was as if her mind had been anesthetized.

She did not actually sleep, but her state was such that she felt little and knew little until the dawn light crept into the room.

Then she looked around in amazement. How could a room be so garishly ugly? The grey light brought out all the ancient grime on the faded wallpaper. The ceiling light was still on and drooled a sickening yellow illumination down over the walls and over her naked body as she lay on the bed. She looked down at herself and saw a small body that seemed to be dotted with bruises.

The evening before came back to her with tremendous impact. Again she saw the parade coming through the door, the barber first, the hardware merchant last. And her vitals writhed in disgust. Not with her victimizers, but with herself. She remembered now how Tom had left her. She remembered the starved arch of her body, she remembered the screaming hunger in her loins. She remembered the men coming, one by one, and she remembered her own outstretched, welcoming arms, the strength of them, the clutch and the strangling grip.

Her body felt as if it had been submerged in a cesspool. Filthy and contaminated and sick inside ...

Later, she phoned downstairs for room service. The smirking bellhop cringed at her sharp demand for food and drink. Not too much food. But plenty of drink. Whiskey ...

Thus the day passed. By five o'clock Lula was pretty drunk. She had consumed her first bottle and was well on her way through the second. If she had attempted such a feat two days before, she would have been deadly ill after the first pint, but now the stuff only strengthened her and buoyed up her nerves. Her capacity was unlimited. She was only *pretty* drunk. After a fifth and a half that was the only state she had attained. She was *pretty* drunk!

She had had nothing but her ham-and-eggs breakfast to eat and she was beginning to consider the possibilities of getting something else when a timid scratch sounded at her door.

For a long time she just sat there, staring at the door, then she murmured, "Come in."

The door opened and Tom stood there.

She stared at him as though he were a ghost. For eons she stared at him. The silence was unbearable.

He stepped inside the door and closed it behind him. He stayed there, against the wall right beside the door and looked at Lula. She did not move. She raised her glass to her lips and took another sip.

When Tom spoke, his voice seemed to come from the depths of his diaphragm. "Lula," he said, "Lula, I … I couldn't stay away …"

She smiled. A horrible, thin, twisted smile. "I can't blame you," she croaked, "I'd have come around myself, under the circumstances, to see if there was anything left."

"Please, Lula, don't!" He rushed across the floor and threw himself down before her, burying his head in her lap. "Forgive me! Please, Lula, forgive me!" His cry was like a child's. "I didn't know what I was doing! I was drunk!"

They said nothing for a long, long while. Finally she began to talk.

"It isn't that I blame you, Tom," she said. "I asked for it. I don't know why I asked for it. Everything seemed so sick, so sordid last night. It's worse today. Where do I go now? What do I do now? My stripping isn't at all what everyone seems to think it is. It's a job. That's all. I am not ashamed of my body. Not now, anyway. Not since I have gotten used to it. I am proud of it, can't you understand that? But they all think I'm something awful because I take my clothes off in public. I am even ashamed myself of the fact that I like it." She paused for a moment. "Yes, I like it. I like to be looked at, to be admired. I like being able to arouse men. Is that so wrong? Who am I hurting?"

Tom said, "Yourself right now."

"That's not because of that. It is because I deliberately dragged myself in the mud last night, after my parents had shoved me into the gutter. But I discovered something. Once you're in the gutter, it is very hard to get out again. You won't let yourself get out. You rub your nose in the filth. It's defiance … or … or something," she finished weakly. Then she laughed. "Have a drink!"

He drank with her and they sat in silence again. Then he spoke quietly.

"I love you, Lula. I will do anything to make up for last night. Please, I am begging you, please marry me. I'll take you away. We'll start over."

She looked at him, then she smiled and glanced around the room with great ostentation. "Where's your white charger, Sir Knight?" she asked bitterly.

"I did this to you, Lula. I want to make it right."

"Ain't that noble, though, sir?" she mocked.

"You don't understand, Lula. I want to help you back on your feet again."

Now she laughed out loud. "You overpower me with your solicitude, Tom. You want to help me back on my feet. You! Are you sorry for the poor, fallen girl? How patronizing can you get?"

"That's not what I meant," he said lamely.

"That's what it sounded like. Thank you just the same, Mr. Burke. I don't need your help. I am not lost. I am confused, and at the present moment, a little sick of myself. Please don't fancy yourself, in the dark night reaching down your lily white hand to lift the fallen woman to her feet as she crouches there before you in humility and shame. I have had too much whiskey to stand that. I may vomit."

"You're just scourging yourself, Lula," he said wearily.

She looked up, eyes blazing. "Damn you!" she cried desperately. "You started it. I was sitting here minding my own business. You came bursting in here and started this whole thing. I didn't invite you. I didn't come crawling to you and ask for comfort. If you don't like it, you can just take off again!"

They said nothing for a long time again. At last, he dropped on his knees before her.

"Lula," he said urgently, "Lula, please believe me, from that first time I had a date with you and took you to Waterworks Hill I have never forgotten you. I rooted for you every time you tried another part in another play. I begged the powers that be that you might have success. I prayed that all your wishes and all your dreams would come true. You paid no attention to me. You ran from me. I wished you nothing but the best. Your life and your career and your success were in my mind and in my heart all the time. 1 know that you never knew this or even dreamed it. But it was so, all the same. That things did not work out quite as you hoped they would when you were the successful college actress, has nothing to do with anything. It has not changed my feeling for you. What happened last night was some kind of weird perversion which I cannot explain and which I won't even try to explain. It has nothing to do with the fact that I have loved you since the first day I saw you and that I still love you and that I will always love you. Please, Lula, please forgive whatever part I had in this mess and open your arms and let us make a brand new start."

She looked at him. "I can't make a brand new start," she sobbed. "I loathe myself, and I am sick with myself for what I did last night. Oh Tom, it is not your fault. It is not mother's and dad's fault. I don't know where the blame lies, if it lies anywhere. Oh, I'm so confused."

She put her arms out and clamped them around his neck and buried her head in his shoulder and wept as if her heart were breaking.

He picked her up in his arms and laid her down gently. He knelt beside her and cradled her head in his arms and rocked her and soothed her and murmured to her and wept with her.

"I love you, Lula, pretty Lula. Dear, pretty Lula."

The days and the nights went by like beads on a string, one like the other, the same, the eternally, everlastingly same. The pain did not let up, nor the remorse, nor the shame. The only release lay in the soothing arms of Tom, who had almost given up his business in his unceasing attempt to make life bearable for Lula again. He shunned his friends of the fateful night and they shunned him.

The episode was never mentioned openly in Centerville, but Lula's parents heard of it somehow and so did everyone else in the little town. An aura of shame hung over the streets and gardens and alleys. Somehow, the town felt the real guilt for what had happened to the girl when she had come home. It knew that it could have met her halfway and turned the homecoming into a joyous thing, but instead it had chosen to strike her down because she was different. It felt the ancient guilt which goes clear back to the primitive village that has just killed a "foreigner." People began shunning Lula's parents and the time came when even her mother and father recognized their share of the guilt. They tried to phone Lula where she was shut up in the hotel, but she would not talk to them.

Tom was the only person in Centerville who laid eyes on Lula during the week that followed. When he was seen on the street he was avoided, not so much through blame as through shame. When the next week's meeting of the Rams Club came around only a few turned up, and they sat around desolately and went home early. The one thing they wanted to get off their chests, they couldn't talk about and it so filled their minds that there was nothing else to say. The barber, the hardware merchant, the clothing salesman and the others who had been involved in the affair were conspicuous by their absence.

Even the boys in the poolroom clicked their balls and cues in somber silence, now and then broken by a forced witticism. But the subject on their minds was never mentioned.

Only the bartender in the old hotel bar went about his business as usual. He felt no guilt. He simply shrugged his shoulders and recognized the foibles of fools.

At the Brunswick Theatre Luke Lucas went about his business. So did Little Jack and Pee Wee and Joe Pastelli. So did Margot and her handsome husband Frank. They had had no word from Lula since she had left.

The show suffered considerably by her absence and the houses dropped off. Joe was frantic. Several times he called the hotel in Centerville to try to entice Lula back to work, but she refused to talk to him. Then he tried all sorts of stunts to trap the trade again. During the time Lula was gone, a constant parade of specialty strippers passed across the Brunswick's stage only to disappear into the outer Siberia of the nightclub trade again. Nothing and nobody seemed capable of replacing the tremendous hit the combination of Lula and Margot had made. Joe saw his huge investment pouring down the drain and he literally wept over the loss of his good money. Each morning he prayed to whatever gods he recognized to bring Lula back before the one o'clock show. But she did not come.

He became almost unbearable as an employer. He cursed his performers and his chorus unmercifully, trying desperately to spur them on to such inhuman efforts as would bring back the crowds. He stood morosely by the box office, reviling the little trickle of customers that seeped into his theatre. He almost whipped an usher for letting in three little boys one afternoon, and promptly fired him when the young man replied that as the show was now, it couldn't possibly hurt a child.

He hardly ever spoke to Margot and when he did it was with biting sarcasm. She was ready to quit, but she knew she could not afford to break her contract.

The Brunswick was just pure hell in those days and through the flames that licked against the ancient, painted scenery walked Luke, thinking his own thoughts and laying his own plans. He was certain that something awful had befallen Lula in her home town and he had been trying madly to figure out a way in which he could help her. Finally, after considering all sorts of possibilities, he arrived at the straightforward scheme of simply going to Centerville and bringing her back. He was elated at his own brilliance and went to Joe Pastelli at once to promote a three day leave of absence in which to carry out his intention.

The producer laughed at him. A certain hysteria had crept into the usually good-natured laugh of Joe and he sounded a little frightening. All the same, Luke persisted in the face of such protests as, "This isn't white slavery! You can't force a girl to perform against her will!"

Luke looked innocent. "Who said anything about her performing?" he wanted to know. "I just want to get her out of the lion's den."

Joe was outraged. "You bring her back here, do you understand? If you get her to leave that little hick hole, you bring her here. She owes me the remainder of a three months contract!"

Luke's eyes widened. "But you just said …"

"I don't care what I said. Are you trying to throw my own words up against me?"

Luke carefully packed his suitcase that night after the last show and the next morning he headed west. His mind was full of misgivings. He loved the blonde stripper as he had never loved anyone before. But somehow he was not so sure that this entitled him to interfere with her life.

There were no misgivings in Joe Pastelli's mind. After his interview with Luke, he met Margot on the fly-floor stairs. He had no hopes at all that Luke was going to be successful in his mission of mercy and his mind was consumed with bitterness over his loss.

Margot smiled stiffly at him and tried to pass him on her way up the steps, but he stood in her way, snarling and hissing like an injured jaguar.

Mercilessly he imitated her as she had spoken on that fateful day after Lula had left the theatre to return to Centerville. "She'll be back. She'll be back. Once a stripper, always a stripper. She's caught in the trap now."

Margot smiled indulgently. "You sound like a fool, Joe," she said, "like a fool without an ounce of patience."

"You wouldn't care to lay a little bet, would you?" he sneered.

"Hell, yes," she laughed. "Name your own amount."

"A hundred bucks!"

"A hundred it is. Come on down here and we'll give the money to Pee Wee to hold."

They went down the stairs together and found Pee Wee. She only laughed when they placed the two century notes in her palm.

When Luke hit Centerville, he looked around in wonder. Hell, they were all alike, weren't they, these little American towns? Centerville was no different from the little town in Ohio from which he hailed. Lula's home town was the exact replica of every single one of the uncounted little burgs he had hit on his endless trek of the flesh circuit. He hardly needed to raise his eyes to find the hamburger joint across from the station, greasy and smelly and unimaginative like every other hamburger joint he had ever been in. He hardly had to look when he picked up his suitcase and wandered along the single street of town to tick off the stores, the parking meters, the puny-lawned residences, and the unimposing front of the shabby, lethargic hotel which served a constant stream of shabby, lethargic salesmen as a flophouse. He tried to recall the hotels in which he had lived during his years of touring, but he found for the thousandth time that he could not tell one from another. Not one of them had ever seemed like a home. Not one of them had ever been colorful or remarkable or even interesting.

He turned in at the entrance, put his valise down on the floor in front of the ever present desk and sallow clerk and asked for the number of Lula's room.

"She ain't seeing nobody," said the clerk laconically.

"She's seeing me."

"If she is, you're the first one besides Tom Burke she has seen in over a week."

"Who's Tom Burke?"

The clerk looked quizzically at Luke. "You a stranger in town?"

"What do I look like?"

"Yeah, I figured you was. Well, she ain't seein' nobody." The man turned away and started to sort mail into the small pigeon-holes behind him.

Luke leaped over the desk and grabbed him by the scruff of the neck. "Do you want me to go up the stairs and yell her name up and down the halls? What's her room number?"

The sallow figure cringed. "Jeez, you don't have to get tough. It's 34. ... but it ain't no use. She won't open the door." He yelled the last part after Luke as he sprinted through the lobby and up the stairs.

Hotel stairs and halls are all alike. Three feet of maroon carpet, lining worn, unpainted steps. Cavernous halls that seem to lead to nowhere in the hushed, upper regions of nothing, echoing with the soft murmurs of clinking glasses, muted laughter, and carefully subdued squeals of feminine throats.

Luke leaped up the stairs and slowed down with every step achieved.

What was he doing here? What right did he have to interfere in Lula's life? His nostrils were filled with the musty odor of washed-out hotel linen, ancient whiskey smells and faint, wraithlike whiffs of perfume. It was a clean smell and an ancient, dead, dust-filled smell all at the same time. He had smelled that identical odor so many times. He could not help but think of Lula, reclining on a bed in one of these rooms, her nostrils filled with the same, slumlike smell.

He slowed down in his ascent. He had a hard time picturing the girl he loved in such cheap, sordid surroundings. Then he shrugged and smiled a little to himself. Who the hell was he that he should consider the atmosphere surrounding the girl of his heart? He had not been too choosy himself in the matter of environment in his own life.

He reached the third floor and stopped at the head of the stairs. For a long time he listened, as if he expected to hear her voice calling for help, but he heard nothing. Actually, he supposed, he had not expected to hear anything, but somehow he had hoped that her voice would have been echoing through the silence, calling his name, begging for his assistance.

Again he laughed a little at himself and went down the hall looking for the number on the door. Presently, he found it. Thirty-four. Later, he remembered that the numerals were painted on the panel with some kind of luminous paint that seemed to burn itself into the wood.

For a long time he stood staring at the number. Then he raised a slow hand and knocked.

There was no answer.

He knocked again and a soft voice—Lula's voice—from within inquired, "Who is it?"

He said, "It's Luke, Lula."

There was silence for quite a while. Then her voice came through the door. "Go away, Luke. Go away."

"I'm not going anywhere," he said, and he stood his ground right there outside her door. "I want to talk to you."

"I don't want to talk to you, so please go away."

He leaned against the door and waited, but no further word came from inside. Finally he said, "I'll be here in the morning so you might just as well let me in now."

He heard the stirring inside and he heard the whispered conversation. Then the door opened a little and she stood before him, more beautiful than he had even remembered she was. "What do you want?" she whispered.

"I want you. I want you to get out of here and go with me."

"I can't," she said.

"Why not?"

"Why should I? What have you got to offer?"

He stared at her. "What do you mean, what have I got to offer?" he asked in amazement. "What kind of a question is that?"

"Why should I go with you?"

"Because I love you, you damned fool," he spluttered. "That's why." Then he looked long at her. "What's happened to you in this little burg? You didn't used to talk like this."

She started to close the door. "Go away."

But he put his feet in it and thought of a whole heritage of brush salesmen who had done the same, and felt like a fool. But he could not keep himself from doing it. He had come a long way to see to it that Lula was all right and he was not getting anywhere. Who was inside this squalid little room with her? Why did she talk as she did?

He pushed his way into the room and stopped just inside the door. "Well," he said, "well ... have we got any liquor in this joint?"

Lula squashed herself against the wall behind him and the half-dressed man on the bed sat up slowly. "It's on the table by the bathroom door," he said slowly. "Help yourself."

"I will, thanks," said Luke. "What're we drinking with it? Soda or water?"

"Water, you bastard," said the man dispassionately.

Luke looked at him. "Do *you* have a name, too?" he asked.

"It's none of your damned business," said the man.

"Well," said Luke, "ain't we chummy?"

He went to the bathroom and fixed himself a drink and when he returned to the room, they were both dressed. He sat in a chair against the wall and watched the two of them. "What the hell do you think you're doing?" he asked.

The man rose to his feet. He was a formidable man. "Look, you little jerk," he said.

Luke shuddered visibly. "You're being damned impolite," he said. "Please, sir, my mother warned me against language like that."

The big man stirred angrily and Lula said, "Please, Tom, no! Luke is a friend of mine."

Luke bowed formally. "You flatter me, fair damsel. If this gorilla wants to start something, let him."

She turned to him and pleaded, "No, Luke, please, no. Tom has been good to me."

Luke wanted to know, "How good?"

"He's my friend."

"I bet. I just bet. I bet he's a real good friend. It's written all over him. How good a friend is he?"

Then she ran to him and she put her hands on him and cried, "I'm so glad to see you, Luke. So glad."

He looked up at her, his watery drink in one hand. "I bet you are," he said drily.

"I am. Honest I am!"

"How glad?"

"Everything has been awful ..."

She was interrupted by Tom. "Not that bad, honestly now, Lula. They haven't been that bad."

"Awful ... just awful!" And she stood before him, twisting her housecoat between her fingers and told him the whole story. In the middle of the recounting, Tom went into the bathroom, apparently bored with the tale, and fixed himself another drink. Then he came out, very nonchalant and perched on the bed, sipping from the glass in his hand. Luke did not take his eyes from him. He heard the story to the end and his guts turned slowly over within him.

"Yeah, yeah, never mind," he said as she was drawing to a close, "I know it all. I know everything there is to be known about these sanctimonious little towns where they have such a tough time stomaching girls like you. Don't tell me any more. I have something to say to our little friend over there on the bed."

Tom looked up. "Watch what you're doing, mountebank," he said oratorically, obviously proud of himself for having thought of such a theatrical term of insult.

But he did not get much of a chance to finish his triumph, for suddenly Luke was all over him. He pulled the big man to his feet and smashed his fist into his jaw.

Tom reeled back in surprise and Lula screamed.

"This is going to be fun," Luke muttered between his teeth and his slum experience came to the fore as he smashed the side of his open hand against Tom's jugular vein, before the bigger man had a chance to recover.

He looked down at his collapsing, retching opponent with some satisfaction. Then, deliberately, he raised his right fist and brought it brutally down on the back of his neck. He heard the heavy thud and saw the head slam against the floor.

He stood there shakily and looked down at the twitching figure. He raised his right foot and slammed it against the fallen man's ribs. Tom cried out and then he laid still. Luke watched him for a long time. Then he was satisfied that no more trouble was to be expected from that quarter.

He turned to Lula. "Pack your things," he said breathlessly. "Pack 'em and let's get out of here. We're going back where we came from."

She started to protest.

"Come on," he said. "Get going."

The first thing Lula saw when she stepped off the train at Grand Central was a flock of reporters. She tried to hide behind Luke, but the horde had seen her and came sweeping down on her like a pack of dogs.

"Miss Lang! Oh, Miss Lang!"

"We heard you were coming back!"

"Where have you been all this time?"

"How about a statement for the press?"

Luke tried to protect her, but it was no use. They thronged around her and would not let her go.

"How about the new winter fashions? Any statement?"

"How about free love?"

"How about the profession of stripping? Any statement about how you feel when you are taking your clothes off?"

"How about a statement about the government scandals?"

"When are you opening again? Where?"

"How about a statement?"

"A statement ... a statement ... a statement."

She did not know what to say. She looked around helplessly and murmured a little to this questioner, a little to that one, knowing full well that the evening papers would be full of the shallow, foolish pronunciamentos generally accredited to show-girls the world over who supposedly think with nothing but their pelves.

Then, through the throng surrounding her excitedly, she saw the approach of Joe Pastelli and Margot. The reporters spied them, too, and abandoned her to cluster around the new arrivals.

Margot put her arms around Lula and smiled her most enig-matic smile for the benefit of the news photographers. Lula shud-dered in her embrace and yet she felt somehow at home. This was where she belonged now. Her college days, her dreams and ideals were all behind her. These were her people. This was her world. The awful experience in Centerville slid behind her and she began to brighten. She even gave Margot a little hug and the woman turned hot, eager eyes on her. A warmth was creeping over Lula, a sense of belonging, a feeling of having found her harbor and being safe. She smiled and joined Joe Pastelli with the reporters.

Joe was in fine form. As the most famous and successful pro-ducer of burlesque left in the United States, he expressed opinions on everything from the Brannan Plan (of which he had heard only vaguely, though he did know it had something to do with corn, a subject upon which he was an expert) to Nehru (who, as far as he knew, was an Indian, although just what kind of Indian was a moot question. A Sioux, perhaps?). He *did* say emphatically that now that Lula was back he would soon present the public with the most lavish, the most expensive, the most sensational burlesque show this nation had ever seen. In his enthusiasm he even mentioned the possibility of staging a comeback for Helen of Troy.

Lula felt fine now. She laughed at Joe's witticisms. She tucked her hand under his arm as they went through the cavernous station to his car. To his anxious questioning as to when she was returning to work, she answered that she would be ready within a day or so. She had come home. She was wanted. It was a good feeling after her week in Centerville.

The party stopped at a bar on its way to Lula's apartment. They had a triumphant drink together and then parted company with mutual assurances that Lula and Joe and Margot would get together on the following day in order to discuss the continuation of the original show.

Luke accompanied Lula home through the canyons of the city. She wanted to walk. She wanted to absorb the sounds and smells of the town which she now considered home. It was like a kind of exile, since she had been rejected in Centerville, but it was home all the same.

When they got to her apartment she threw open the door and cried out with abandoned pleasure as she entered the familiar rooms. She opened all the windows and wandered from one to another of the three rooms, looking lovingly at her furniture and touching each piece with her hands. Then she went to the little kitchen and produced a bottle of Scotch. She poured two generous drinks and brought one to Luke who was standing forlornly in the center of the living room.

"Here's to the Brunswick," she cried. "Here's to you and me and the whole topsy-turvy world!" She took a deep draught from her drink and flopped herself on the couch, clutching the glass firmly in her hand.

Luke sat down on the edge of a chair. He looked at her and at her synthetic comfort for quite a while before he spoke. "Are you really going back to work at the Brunswick?"

She looked her surprise. "Certainly. Why not?"

"It hasn't brought you much happiness."

"What has that got to do with it? I didn't expect it would when I went into it. After all, it was not what I had intended."

"I beg you, please, no matter how Joe flatters you or Margot urges you, don't do it. Please don't do this to yourself."

"Do what to myself?"

"What you're apparently bent on doing." She started to protest, but he interrupted her. "No, listen to me. I know what you're going to say. You're going to protest that you don't know what I am talking about. But deep down you know perfectly well what is on my mind. Through desperation and through generosity to your parents, you got yourself into a profession that now has branded you as an outcast among the people whose opinions you respect … your home folks. Lord, Lula, we've all got home folks. I've got 'em, too. What do you think they say about my being a burlesque comedian? I wouldn't care to repeat it and it is something I find very hard to live with. Now you've got a perfect way out. Don't go back to it. Get a job selling or waiting on tables or *anything,* but don't go back to something that will never bring you anything but misery."

She stared at him. "But you said yourself that this sort of thing is only a stopgap."

"Sure, sure, for a comedian, but what kind of a stopgap is it for you? Do they strip on TV? Do they strip in legit? You'll be branded. Is that what you want?"

"No, it isn't. But I don't think you're necessarily infallible in your ideas on the subject."

"I'm sorry, Lula. I don't suppose I am. All I know is that I love you."

She laughed at that and he got furious. He jumped to his feet and cried angrily, "Don't laugh at me, Lula. What a hell of a moment to choose to laugh!"

"I'm sorry, Luke. I'm more sorry than I can tell you. I don't know what came over me. It's just that I have heard that phrase too often during the last few days. It seems that every time a man wants a girl to follow his advice, he invokes his love for her."

"I'm not invoking anything. I was telling you the truth. If you don't care to listen to it, I can't force you."

"That wasn't what I meant either, Luke. I *know* you love me and I am grateful for it, but the fact that you love me does not make you an oracle as far as my destiny is concerned. Believe me, I know that I am defiant right now. I know that I want to show 'em. I know that I am full of bitterness and cynicism. But I think I also know what I am doing. I did not mean to laugh at your love. It was the condition under which it was mentioned that I laughed at, and I apologize for that."

Suddenly, it occurred to her that he had never even kissed her yet. She offered her warm mouth willingly and he held her close. The kiss lasted a long, satisfying time.

After it was over and he reached a little breathlessly for his drink, she smiled gently and said, "All right. There, now. It is official. It has been sealed. All the same I want to pursue my own path in my own way. Is that understood?" He nodded glumly and she continued. "I know what is worrying you, Luke, and I understand it, knowing also how you feel about me, but I can't help it. You see ..." she hesitated for a long while, "... you see, I love what I am doing."

She waited for retort, but he just stared at her and she went on. "Yes, I love it. I get a thrill out of it. I know that is hard to believe since you saw me that very first time. But all the same, that was when I discovered it. I guess I'm just what they call an exhibitionist. I get an enormous thrill out of my work. I discovered *that* the very first time I did it, even while I was having such an awful time. It grew on me during the times that followed, and I have actually missed it, even though it has cost me so much misery. It never occurred to me that this was what I was cut out for. A girl coming from my sort of background does not take naturally to that kind of thing. If anyone had even mentioned the possibility to me I would have been horrified at the notion. So would my family and all my former friends. As a matter of record, they *are* horrified, as we know only too well. But now I have broken away from the past and this is my life and I love it."

Luke said, "You never break away from your past."

"We'll see."

"Please don't do it, Lula," he begged. "What will it get you?"

"A number of things I want. Money, excitement, my name in lights, fame ..."

"Notoriety, you mean."

"You're a fine one to talk; you're in it yourself."

"What are you trying to prove, Lula?"

"I'm not sure," she said softly. "But whatever it is, I can't stop now ..."

CHAPTER SEVEN

There was probably not a single hep-cat in the auditorium, but that bass drum was strictly for hep-cats. It boomed and rocked through the boogie-woogie tempo as if it had a personality all its own.

The girls, better now at the Brunswick than they used to be, slid through their routine, their short green skirts and scarlet blouses swinging and jiving. The jitterbug team did its stuff, the girl's legs whirling free in the air and the boy's hands clutching her breasts in the barrel-rolls. It was strictly hot. It was successful and it brought the customers' hands together in a crashing avalanche.

The curtain swung shut, screeching and swirling on its giant track. The orchestra struck up *Sweet Adeline* and the front curtain opened again, revealing a moth-eaten town square with a fountain in the middle ... all painted on the act-curtain which billowed slightly in the air conditioning.

(Luke and Little Jack enter from stage left. They are carrying a pint bottle and are singing lustily "Sweet Adeline.")

JACK: Wait a minute, wait a minute, you'll never get in the opera that way.

LUKE: Who wants to get in the opera. I want to see a girlie show.

JACK: No, I mean you'll never get a job singing in the opera. You must practice. That's a terrible "A" you've got there.

LUKE: Your "A" ain't so pretty, either.

(*They stop by the painted fountain and Luke pantomimes taking swig from bottle and washing it down with water from the fountain. Jack takes him by the coat tail.*)

JACK: Here now, that's enough drinking, let's hear you sing.

LUKE: (*Goes into a caterwauling version of "Sweet Adeline."*)

JACK: Oh, no! That's awful. Your *pizzicato* is trembling too much.

LUKE: (*Looks down his front and tries a note or two*) It is shaking a little, ain't it?

JACK: Now listen to me. (*He takes a big swig and tries a few notes.*)

(*A big cop enters from stage right, swinging his club menacingly.*)

COP: Here, here, just a minute. Can't you two read?

(*Jack and Luke stop singing and look malignantly at the cop.*)

JACK: We're singing by ear.

COP: (*Pointing to backdrop which displays a big sign saying* HOSPITAL! QUIET!) Can't you read that sign? It says HOSPITAL! QUIET! No singing here! (*He starts out at left, and Jack and Luke, after quick swigs, burst into song again. The cop stops and comes back, menace written all over him.*)

COP: Now quit that, do you hear? One more sound out of you under that hospital sign and I'll run you in.

LUKE: We'll move over. (*They move over to the other side of the stage, and after quick swigs burst into song once more. The cop is furious. He swings his club and steps close to them.*)

COP: All right! You asked for it. I'm running you in. (*He moves between Luke and Jack and takes each by an arm and starts off with them, but Jack stops him.*)

JACK: (*Passing bottle behind cop's back to Luke who takes a quick swig while Jack is talking and then when the cop turns* to him, passes it back to Jack who drinks while Luke is talking, and so on, back and forth, until the bottle is empty.) Officer, you can't mean it! Would you run in the latest and finest opera star in America?

COP: (*Turns to Luke in amazement*) This? An opera star?

LUKE: Yes. The name is Rigoletto.

COP: (*Turns to Jack*) Rigoletto?

JACK: Yeah, beautiful name, ain't it?

COP: (*Turns back to Luke*) What's your full name?

LUKE: Rigoletto Mortis.

COP: Well, let's hear you sing.

(*Luke opens his mouth, but not a sound comes out. Jack coughs violently and as cop turns toward him questioningly, he passes bottle to Luke who puts it to his mouth, but it is empty. He signals frantically to Jack and coughs violently himself. As cop turns back to Luke, now staring in consternation from one to the other, Jack lifts a small half-pint bottle from cop's back pocket, holds it up to the light, sees it is almost full and passes it behind cop's back to Luke, who takes a deep swig and bursts forth into glorious song, passing the bottle back to Jack as the cop turns to listen. Jack has a deep swig, washes his mouth out with the liquid and swallows it with obvious enjoyment. From the looks of his admiring glances at the bottle, it must be at least ten-year-old Scotch. Jack listens to Luke in amazement and holds the bottle up for closer inspection. Luke warbles on in fine voice. The cop is impressed.*)

COP: Well, well, that's fine. All the same, no singing in front of the hospital.

(*Jack, who has had another swig, bursts forth in song himself. He too now has a gorgeous voice. Luke listens in amazement, reaches for bottle and drinks deeply, then he drops bottle back in cop's pocket.*)

COP: Say, are you a singer, too?

JACK: (*Astounded*) I guess I am. (*He sings.*) I never knew I was. (*He sings.*) Oh boy, can I sing! (*He howls triumphantly like wolf.*)

COP: All right, that's enough now. No more noise and disturbance.

(*Jack and Luke, at the top of their glory, throw their arms around each other and sing beautifully in harmony.*)

LUKE AND JACK: Wow! Listen to us! We're singers! We'll get rich!

COP: (*Puzzled*) What's the matter with you two? I thought you said you were singers in the first place.

JACK: Officer, we cannot lie to you. We said we were singers. But we really were not. We were just drinking and got to singing, but Officer, while you were talking to us, we stole some whiskey from the bottle in your back pocket and it turned us into real singers. Please, officer, tell us what kind of whiskey that is, so we can drink it all the time and get to be famous singers.

COP: (*Laughs uproariously*) Whiskey! Whiskey? That wasn't whiskey you drank, it's a specimen my wife asked me to drop off at the hospital!

(BLACKOUT)

Lula had hated that skit from the first time she saw it. It always turned her stomach. She could see nothing even remotely funny in it and she could not understand the guffaws from the audience.

Not that she cared. She sat in her dressing room, nursing a long, cool drink, listening to the show on the monitor system, waiting for her cue to come for her last bit of the evening.

This was the new Lula. There was a hardness and a brittleness about her now that belied her twenty-two years. She was wearing too much make-up, and when she looked in the mirror, she hated her face for it. The well-mannered college girl was gone. Her gentleness, her idealism, her dreams were gone. And left was only a hard shell that had gradually become harder and harder during the long month since she had come back.

She had thrown herself into her work with an energy that thrilled Joe Pastelli to the core. By practicing diligently day after day, she had achieved a mastery over her work unparalleled by anyone in the business. She had evolved three new acts for herself, ranging from the purely innocent to the torridly sultry. She had received one offer after another for appearances in other theatres and in nightclubs, but so far she had declined them all.

Her face and figure and name had become famous along Broadway and in the fashionable bistros. Her name appeared again and again in the columns, now linked with this playboy and now with that. It seemed almost as if she worked hard at getting her name in the papers, as if she could not do enough to remind her folks back home of what she was doing. Her whole attitude most of the time was one of half-sullen defiance.

It had not taken her long to lose her personal popularity. A few surly remarks and an occasional irritated rejoinder had done it in no time. The rest of the company avoided her now, with the exceptions of Margot and Luke. The former seemed amused at the developments, the latter was heartbroken. But Lula paid no attention to either of them. She went her own way and chose her own company from among the moneyed gentry of the night.

There was a running bet among the girls in the chorus as to how many of her innumerable dates had enjoyed her intimate favors. But the fact of the matter was that not a single one of them had. She had had her fill of that sort of thing in Centerville and she seemed to take a cruel pleasure in leading them to expect the ultimate and then denying them when the moment came.

She was making a lot of enemies. Not many men mind terribly being refused by a girl, but all of them hate to be led by the nose into expectation and *then* to be refused. There was a lot of talk about her, but such was her glamor and her tremendous success on the stage that, no matter how much their friends warned them, there were always plenty of new suitors at her door.

The troupe thought that success had turned her head. But it was not her head that was turned.

It was her heart.

She leaned her elbows on the dressing-table and sat staring at her face in the mirror. It seemed to her that through the heavy pancake make-up, she could see the furrows of the slut in Centerville. She caught up the little foam rubber pad and rubbed some more of the stuff on her face, but through the make-up the deepening creases of harlotry still showed. She smeared her face frantically, putting the quick-drying goo on in great, thick streaks. But it still showed. The bitterness and the hardness and the burning disappointment ...

She dropped her face in her hands for a moment, then returned to her drink.

There was a knock at her door, but she did not answer it. It was opened gently and Hansel Schnitzler came in. He closed the door carefully behind him and stood just inside it by the wall, looking at her.

"Hello, little chicken," he said.

She did not turn around. "Rat," she said, very quietly.

"Now, now, now. What's this? A mood?"

She still did not raise her voice. "What do you want, you fat, disgusting freak?"

Hansel clucked despairingly and eased himself into a chair by the door. As he straddled it, it disappeared under his enormous bulk. "Oh now, really," he said, "I've lost weight. My doctor says so. He put me on yogurt. Ever tried it? What a way to start a day off." He rambled on. "I used to dream of being slim and athletic like a young Greek ... I dreamed of being renowned for my personal beauty." He shrugged elaborately. "Oh well, you can always buy beauty."

"You can't buy me," she gritted between her teeth.

"Oh now, girlie, who ever mentioned such a thing?" He smiled gently. "Of course, there *are* reports going about, dealing rather intimately with your private life."

She turned on him furiously. "You can't do a thing to me! Not a thing!"

"Now Lula, why would I want to do a thing to you? You're my bread and butter, darling. Handling you has turned into quite a proposition."

"You earned it," she muttered. "After all, you started me in the business."

"Yes, I did, didn't I? I pride myself on recognizing latent talent when I see it."

"All right. You've gotten that off your chest. Now go away and leave me alone."

He looked at her for a long time. "What a difference," he sighed. "Do you remember the little, scared girl who shook and trembled in my office?"

"I remember her. I remember her only too well."

"Well, she's come quite a way since then, hasn't she? And now I can bring her good news. Good offers. We can hardly afford to keep turning them down."

"I'm not going anywhere. I like it here."

"But this is money, dearie. Real money, not the chicken feed we're making here."

"You mean *I'm* making, don't you?"

"You put things so bluntly, honey. I have not been useless to you."

"Bloodsucker."

Hansel was getting angry. "Look, chicken, I made you. I can break you. I've got enough on you to fill a book. Don't be such a prima donna with me."

"Break me if you think you can. Go ahead. If our relationship is going to be one continual line of threats and recriminations, what do I want to go on for in the first place?"

Hansel had gone too far and he knew it. "Well, we'll talk business later. Business is so unpleasant. How about supper with me?"

"No."

"You have to eat."

"Right, but I can still choose my company."

He shrugged. "Have it your own way," he said and rose to leave. But just then there was a knock at the door again.

"Come on in," she said, and Hansel, with elaborate manners, opened the door.

Frank Powell stood there.

Tito's Restaurant, fashionable as it was, always had about it an aura of a hash-joint. It was always noisy and it always stank of cooking. Some people regarded this as a virtue. It made them feel at home. It whetted their appetites. Frank hated the smell and he frequented Tito's only because the owner was an unfailing source of the kind of gossip which was grist for Frank's mill.

That evening, he had met Margot there for supper. This was something else he hated, for wherever Margot went she was recognized. Frank loathed the notoriety and the lack of privacy. And he hated being addressed as "Mr. Diego."

He tried to steer Margot off into a quiet, unobtrusive corner, but reticence was not one of the stripper's virtues, and she plunked herself down at a table in the direct center of the room, basking in the stares and half-whispered comments. Then she turned to Frank.

"Let's eat," she said, "I've got something I want you to do."

One of Tito's immaculate waiters came over and she ordered a meal that would have done a plowhand proud. Frank, sitting there across the table from her, was a little amazed at his capacity for disliking almost everything about Margot while still remaining her willing slave. Her almost unlimited vulgarity, apparent only to people who knew her well enough to eat with her and share a bathroom or a bedroom with her, repulsed every instinct of refinement in him. Deep inside him was an imbedded hankering for daintiness and gentleness in his woman, and seeing this one gobble down huge amounts of roast beef and cabbage and potatoes, washing it down with schooners full of beer, revolted him. It was almost impossible for him to eat with her. He ordered a Manhattan and mumbled something about dining later.

"You never eat," she said, as her face emerged from the foam of her first schooner of beer. She belched without attempting to conceal it. "How in the hell you survive without eating is something I'll never know." She looked longingly toward the kitchen, but her dinner was not forthcoming as yet. She dug into her purse, causing a cloud of powder to emerge from its gaping maw. Finally she found what she was looking for. A lipstick. She applied it generously to her beautiful mouth, and sighing contentedly, settled back in her chair.

Frank looked with loathing at the edge of her beer mug. It already had a thick coating of lipstick on it. He thought of the glasses in their home which invariably were so covered with lipstick around the rims that it was impossible to wash them clean. He wondered how he was able to stand her.

But he knew why he could stand her. He knew why he did not run away from her. He knew what held him. He waited for what it was she wanted to talk to him about.

She started very casually. "We haven't thrown a party for a long time."

"No," he said, watching her intently. "It doesn't seem to me that our relationship has been such that there was much point in partying together."

"Oh Frank, you always sound as if you're trying to put me on the spot. Are you trying to develop some kind of guilt complex in me?"

"No. I just happened to say what I thought."

"Well, what is it you're thinking? Every time we get together, which is rare enough, you seem to be doing nothing but taking sly digs at me. What have I done?"

"Nothing, I guess, from your viewpoint."

"Well then, what have I done from *your* viewpoint?"

Frank stretched his legs nervously under the table and turned and twisted his drink between his fingers. "Oh Margot, it is so complicated I don't know whether I can explain it or not."

"Well, try."

Frank asked suddenly, "Do you love me, Margot?"

The beautiful stripper was amused. "Why Frank, what a funny thing to ask!"

"Why is it so funny? You're my wife."

"All right. I'll try to answer you. I suppose I do love you."

"You suppose?"

"Frank, there are fifty million ways of loving. Do you love me?"

"Never mind about that. Go on with your explanation."

"Well, remember when we were married. I wasn't anybody then."

"Do I remember? Did you love me then?"

"You were tremendously important to me, Frank."

"That's not what I asked." He made a grimace. "Niagara Falls. Was I corny! You must really have been laughing up your sleeve. Was I romantic!"

"You were very sweet, Frank."

"Thank you. I guess I was even sweeter when I did what you wanted in return for marrying me. When I put you on the map. That's what you wanted, wasn't it?"

"Well, I must admit you *did* do me a lot of good in my career."

"Your career."

"Well, what's wrong with it? What a small town boy you are, Frank."

"That's the truth. How I used to dream about the Little Woman! You know that favorite of American advertising pictures, the well-dressed young executive husband coming up the walk toward his green-shuttered, hygienic little home? The front door is open and in the doorway stands his model wife, every hair in place, clean, neat, dainty. Down the walk run two towheaded children, happily gurgling about Daddy being home. Where the hell does this miracle exist?"

"Did you expect to win that by marrying an actress?"

"Actress!" he cried.

"You *can* be insulting, can't you, darling?" He shrugged and slumped into his chair and she continued, "Anyway, what I started to say was simply that at the time we were married, I admit that I was not head-overheels in love with you. How many wives are? They may think they are, but I am allowing myself the luxury of doubting their feelings. When you talk about love, what are you talking about? Physical love? That mythical thing known as *spiritual* love? Or what? If you would go to the trouble of asking around among your married friends, you would probably find them just as puzzled about love as you seem to be. Does it occur to you that it is harder to *like* people than it is to *love* them? And that love in marriage eventually develops into the ability to like the person you share your life with? Isn't that where you feel failure, Frank? You don't like me. At times you love me. Even love me frantically, but you don't like me. Therefore I do not make a good companion for you."

Frank stared at her in open-mouthed amazement.

She continued. "I surprise you, don't I, Frank? You hadn't expected that from me, had you? Well, I'm not completely without brains. I know what it is that ties you to me and I know that it has nothing to do with liking me. I'll surprise you further. I even know what it is that binds me to you. You are practical for me, Frank. You are expedient. I have the inside track on the Great White Way with you as my husband. In return for that I am willing to do certain things for you. And in return for what I do for you, you are willing to put me on the map, as you so quaintly put it. That's a fair bargain, isn't it? Oh, my friend, you would be surprised if you knew how many marriages are based on fair bargains." She laughed.

Frank was appalled. "I never realized the full extent of your cynicism," he muttered. But the truth of what she had said sat in him and rankled.

"That's not cynicism, Frank. Sometimes cynicism attempts to pass itself off as the bitter truth. It almost never is. It is no doubt often bitter, but it is hardly ever truth. What I have been saying is truth."

Her dinner arrived then and she threw herself at it with her usual vigor, but Frank's mind was too occupied with what she had said for him to even notice her violent chewing and swallowing.

At last he looked up. "I admit defeat in the face of your devastating logic," he said. "Margot, I wonder whether you know how many times I have been on the verge of asking for a divorce."

"Oh, I know," she mumbled, her mouth full of food, "those times have usually been the ones when I worked the hardest to give you what you want. I simply could not afford to lose you. That's being honest with you, isn't it?"

"Yes, you're honest, all right."

He ordered a drink and when it came, he drank it quickly and ordered another. Slowly the anesthesia spread through him, and as it spread he became more able to face his disappointment and his real sense of loss. He could even smile at his beautiful wife as he inquired, "What was it you wanted me to do?"

She wiped her mouth on her napkin, smearing wide streaks of purplish red across the white damask, but he did not even wince.

"As I said, I want to throw a little party," she murmured.

"When?"

"Tonight."

"That's awfully quick notice, isn't it?"

"Maybe. But I feel like it tonight."

"OK. What do you want me to do?"

"I want you to ask Lula Lang."

There was a long silence. Then Frank said quietly, "I won't do it."

"Why not?"

"She's a sweet girl, Margot. Nothing doing."

"She's not so sweet any more."

"All the same, the kind of parties you throw … no, I won't do it."

"What's the matter with you? What do you think I want her for?"

"That's exactly what I mean. No, not Lula Lang."

She sat there, looking at him in complete puzzlement. "What's with Lula Lang?"

"Nothing."

"What's between you and her?"

"Margot, she doesn't even know me."

"Then how? … oh …" and realization dawned on her, "that first night at the Brunswick." She leaned back and laughed. "Brother! She must have made *some* impression on you." He did not answer and she went on, "Why haven't you looked her up? Why haven't you dated her? You, who can do so much for strippers?"

He sighed wearily. "You don't know what you're talking about, Margot. You haven't the faintest idea." He started to get up in order to get away from her cat's eyes, piercing into his secret the way they were.

"Sit down," she hissed. "Sit down!" He sank back in his chair and she regarded him with renewed interest.

"Well now, what have we here? Love? Frank Loverboy! Reticent and shy and country bumpkin. What a laugh. What a scream!" She gritted her teeth and regarded him malignantly.

Frank was restless. He moved uncomfortably in his chair under her probing scrutiny.

She spoke quietly. "I want you to go over this evening and ask her to the party, Frank, and no ands, ifs, or buts."

"I won't do it, Margot."

"Are you in love with her, Frank?"

"Mind your own business."

"Well, do as I say, and we'll have a good time." She started to gather her things together, but he remained seated, staring at her, hatred in his eyes. When she saw his hesitation, she stopped. "I think you'll do it, Frank. I hate to remind you, but I could do you a lot of damage."

He was in despair. "Why her, Margot? Why her? There's any number of girls we could party with. Why her?"

She drew on her gloves, obviously feasting on the many eyes that were watching her. "I want *her* particularly, Frank. Most particularly. It should make an interesting evening." She looked at him menacingly. "Do you understand, Frank? I want *her!*"

She turned and walked out of the restaurant. He did not follow her. He sat there, cursing himself for his weakness, for his slavishness. Loathing himself ...

Hansel's face widened into a wide, ingratiating grin. "Well, Mr. Powell," he cried, "come in! Come in!" He stepped back and allowed Frank to enter the room. After that he closed the door and made no move to leave. "And what can we do for you, Mr. Powell?" he inquired genially.

Lula had swung around in her seat and was staring at Frank Powell. So this was the man who had started the whole thing with his column. She did not know whether to laugh or cry at finally seeing him personally. She had known all along, of course, that he was Margot's husband, but she had never mentioned his name and Margot had never said anything about him, either.

She looked at him with interest. He made a handsome figure in his dinner jacket, and Lula was agreeably attracted to him. She had no inclination to blame him for what had happened to her. After all, *she* was the one who had performed. All *he* had done was to praise the performance. He had had no way of knowing what far-reaching effects his column would have.

Now he stood just inside the door, with Hansel hovering over him. He was obviously uncomfortable and Lula was puzzled that this great man, whose single word could make or break a performer, should look so much like a little boy caught stealing a rubber ball in a Five-and-Dime. She stood up and went toward him.

"How do you do, Mr. Powell," she said quietly and extended her hand to him. It seemed to her that there was pain in his eyes as he took her hand, but she dismissed the notion as being preposterous. Why on earth should he be pained?

Hansel seemed about to jump out of his skin. He grabbed Frank by the arm in a rough, rude manner, intended to be solicitous, and dragged him toward a chair. "Here, man," he cried, "sit down! Take a load off! Here, here's a chair!" Frank was practically thrown into a seat and Hansel stood bending over him, rubbing his hands together. "Well, sir," he stuttered in his eagerness, "well, sir, it's a pleasure to see you. And how are you these days?"

The agent was in a veritable dither. Frank Powell was an important man in Hansel's business. The red-carpeted royal treatment was evidently none too good for such a well-syndicated columnist.

Lula said, "I suppose I should thank you for that column you wrote about me."

"Please," Powell answered. "You were beautiful to watch."

She went on. "I don't expect you to realize what havoc that column created in my life."

"I didn't know," he said. "In that case I am very sorry I wrote it, although I still mean every word of it."

Hansel turned effusively toward Lula, now perched again on her dressing-table stool. "Why, baby," he cried, "what's a little trouble? Think of the good it did you."

Lula shrugged her shoulders indifferently.

Hansel carried on. He grabbed a small stool and pulled it out into the middle of the floor until it was directly in front of Frank's chair. Then he sat down on it and the stool seemed to disappear as great folds of his flesh draped down on either side of it. It was revolting to watch and both Frank and Lula averted their eyes. He leaned forward and put a hand on Frank's knee.

"Listen," he said. "Listen, I've got a lot of dirt for you. Lula … that is …" he hesitated dramatically, "… there may be a permanent liaison in Lula's life soon." He leered coyly over his shoulder toward Lula and managed to look like a keg-shaped leprechaun.

Lula almost laughed, he looked so ludicrous, but what he had said kept her from giving in to the impulse. "What are you talking about?" she asked in amazement.

His huge face was a study in archness. "Why, chicken," he cried, "you wouldn't deny me, would you?"

Now Lula did laugh. She laughed loud and long and the sound was not pleasant. At last she caught her breath, but what she had to say was not necessary. She knew that Frank already understood. He must have seen and heard this kind of scene a million times with other dancers and other agents, eager to get their clients' names in his column.

"I'll remember," he said drily, "I'll stop by on my way home and warn the Little Church Around the Corner. I understand they have a long waiting list."

"Hey," said Lula. "You don't really mean this?"

Frank smiled broadly. "Certainly," he said in mock seriousness, "such an occasion should be adequately prepared for."

It had become a joke. Somehow Hansel's grossness and stupidity was no longer revolting. It was almost a little endearing. His eagerness. He was like a Saint Bernard puppy. She felt grateful toward Frank. She was tremendously attracted to him.

Hansel gaped from one to the other, obviously aware that his firecracker had fizzled and not quite understanding why.

Frank stood up and Hansel at once leaped to his feet, if such an elephantine movement could have been considered a "leap." The columnist retreated toward the door. He stood there for a moment, looking at Lula, and he seemed to her again to be like a little boy. An ashamed, shy, uncertain little boy.

"Miss Lang," he stammered.

"Lula," she said. "Just call me Lula."

"Lula," he continued, hesitating ever so slightly over the name, "I did not come here to take up much of your time. It's just that I have been relegated to invite you to a party at my house tonight after the show. That is," he added, "if you are not already engaged."

"Why no, I'd love to come. Thank you."

"Well," he said lamely, "well, fine. Fine. It ... it may be quite a party. Margot ... eh ... that's my wife ..." he added brightly, "eh ... Margot throws some pretty rough ones."

"Oh," she laughed. "You can't scare me away. I'd really love to come."

Powell started toward the door, then stopped suddenly. He turned toward the agent. "You come, too, won't you?" he said. "Safety in numbers, you know." He nodded a quick farewell and left.

Hansel turned toward Lula after the door had closed. "Well," he said. "Well!" He rubbed his hands together. "We're moving in high society. When shall I pick you up?"

"You're not going to pick me up, you big fool," Lula said. She could not find it in herself to get really angry with Hansel. He was such a big, bumbling, stupid, shrewd, clever, moronic ass. "Find yourself a date and bring her."

"But he said for us to come together."

"He didn't say anything of the kind. He said for you to come, too. Get yourself a date. I'll come by myself."

MARK TRYON

It was midnight when Lula arrived at the Powells' apartment in the swank apartment house on Park Avenue. She had taken a taxi in from the Brunswick and had stopped at her own place long enough to change clothes and have a couple of quick ones.

She was in fine shape. Dressed in a cocktail-length golden dress, with her hair piled on top of her head, she did not look as if she had left college behind only a few months before. She looked as if she had been born and brought up on the Gay White Way.

She was a little drunk. Just drunk enough to still the soft voice that kept crying within her. The voice that kept warning her. Just drunk enough to pay it no attention.

Something about this party was all wrong. She knew that. She did not give a damn. No, that was not quite true, she knew. She very much gave a damn, but she refused to pay any heed to the warning that was pounding through her.

It was all a part of her defiance. It was all a part of her new life. She was a little afraid of Margot. More than a little. And still, here she was, attending a party at Margot's home. When she had accepted the invitation, it had seemed to be the thing to do. She wasn't so sure now. There was something about the woman that seemed threatening, somehow.

Lula had never in all her life met anyone like Margot. One moment she seemed so sweet. She would put her arm around Lula and her face so close, and she would seem to be a friend. Then at other times she seemed to be a complete stranger. An enemy, even. She would look out from the corners of those startling eyes of hers and suddenly there would be a malevolent wickedness in the atmosphere.

Even when Margot was friendly, there was something wrong about her. She was not friendly the way other women were friendly. Her hands were too intimate, too caressing. At times she seemed almost as if she were a man. It was bewildering, this strange lust that was in her. Bewildering, and yet somehow—fascinating …

Frank Powell was another matter. He had struck Lula as being an uncommonly attractive man. As a matter of fact, she had a hard time reconciling the fact that the two were married. She had never seen two people more different. Frank was like the men she had been used to before she came to New York and became involved with Joe Pastelli and Hansel and Little Jack Horner. Frank was a gentleman. She knew that such a description would be laughed at in the big city. But that was what he was, all the same. She felt comfortable with Frank. She felt safe.

Just why the warning voice was crying in her was something she could not explain, but as she went up in the elevator her impulse was to turn around and go home and forget that she had ever been invited.

She did not turn around. She left the elevator and crossed the little vestibule and rang the doorbell.

Frank opened the door. From the room behind him came the soaring sound of a Stan Kenton record and the babble of voices. Somehow this reassured Lula. She had not expected to be alone with the Powells. All the same she had been afraid of some sort of intimacy. Just what kind of intimacy she could not have explained, even to herself. It was obvious that there were a lot of people present at the party and the knowledge restored her confidence. She smiled at Frank and he opened the door wide and stood aside for her.

"Welcome to our cave," he said. He did not smile. He stared at her.

There was something odd about that stare too. Lula was beginning to be exasperated with herself. What was the matter with her? She was just going to a party together with the people she worked with. They were going to have a few drinks and then they would go home and tomorrow they would comment on what a good time they had had, and that would be all. She was infuriated with herself for seeing hidden meanings, mystery, and veiled threats in everything.

All the same, Frank's face reflected something beyond the usual bland expression of a conventional host. No smile. No apparent pleasure at seeing her. A kind of tense expectation. Expectation of what? Full of vague misgivings, but mentally trying to shrug them off, she entered the room just as the record stopped playing.

There were six people in the room, including Frank and Margot. The guests were Little Jack Horner and his wife Pee Wee and Hansel Schnitzler who had brought along as his date a very tiny, dazzling blonde, who was sitting on the rug at his feet. The girl looked as if she could not be much older than fifteen or sixteen and there was a strangely depraved aura hovering around her. She seemed much too young to appear so sophisticated. Actually, she was twenty-seven years old, but Lula had no way of knowing that.

No one stood up when she came into the room. It would not have been in character with the kind of people they were. Hands were waved lazily at her. Frank pressed a drink into her hand, his eyes lingering on her face. Eyes that burned and smoldered and disturbed her greatly. Hansel, from his half-reclining position introduced her to the tiny blonde, who looked up briefly with a dazzling, childish smile. Her name was Edith something-or-other. It was a foreign name and Hansel slurred over it, as if he were not quite sure either of the spelling or the pronunciation himself. Then she was sitting in a webbed modernistic chair and had a chance to study the room while another record was playing … a wild, orgiastic piece of music she had never heard before.

In the rapt silence as the others listened to the music she looked around, and what she saw pleased every esthetic instinct in her. The large studio living room was furnished and decorated with exquisite taste. Nothing garish, nothing that reflected any of Margot's vulgarity.

It came to her that Margot was quite disinterested in her home and that the decor was the result of Frank's taste. If Margot had had anything to do with it, it would have been bound to reflect her more than it did.

The room had a large red brick fireplace in which a cheerful fire crackled. On the floor was a thick, luxurious carpet, and the furniture was strictly functional. Spindly, practical, comfortable looking in a light and airy manner. Under the huge picture window which seemed to open out onto a terrace was an enormous desk piled high with papers and newspapers, a typewriter, a dictaphone, and all the other appurtenances of Frank's profession. The lighting was softly furnished by a few strategically placed indirect lamps.

It was a cozy room, an intimate room. Too intimate. It was so intimate that it threatened over-familiarity. Somehow, gentle and warm and comfortable as it was, it had a sinister quality about it.

The record broke off in the unsatisfying screech of an unresolved chord at the end. It had reached an almost mad peak and Lula was amazed to find that the other people in the room were in a tremendous state of tension. That they were trembling, in fact. That they were breathing hard and their eyes were avoiding each other.

Frank's glance flicked over her for a brief second, and then he rose and turned off the record player. "That's enough of that this early in the game," he said. His voice was heavy with a meaning that Lula could not understand.

The others seemed to grasp it, however. They stirred and stretched and Little Jack went to the portable bar beside the fireplace to fix himself another drink. "You know," he said over his shoulder, "it's no wonder they tell such fascinating stories about that composer's private life. Anybody who can write music like that is bound to have run the gamut. They say he was quite a voodooist for a while." Jack laughed harshly. "It seems he was trying to do away with his mother. You know, stuck pins in her effigy and things like that. Mumbo jumbo." He came back and perched on the arm of Pee Wee's chair. She did not look up. She was looking at Frank, who was stirring uncomfortably under her stare.

Jack went on. "I wonder why there's such a hell of a lot of that in this country?" he asked no one in particular. "With one hand we revere our mothers in a perfectly insane and grotesque exaggeration of filial adoration, with the other we snarl at her like wild animals and try our best to destroy her. Not just kill her, but destroy her utterly, grind her in the dirt, smash her, crush her." There was an intensity to his voice that went far beyond anything called for as far as the somewhat casual conversation was concerned.

Lula thought of her own mother and she thought she knew at least part of the answer. She did not speak, however, and was startled when Hansel almost screeched a protest at Little Jack.

"You slob," he cried in a voice that sounded as if he were ten years old. "Talk about your own mother, if you want to …"

Jack grinned unconcernedly. "Who said I was talking about my own mother? I was just talking about mothers in general."

Hansel almost frothed at the mouth. "Well, leave my mother out of it, you dirty rat!" Edith patted his hand and smiled vacantly at him from where she was sitting on the floor. Lula was amazed to see that Hansel was crying, and now he leaned over and buried his face in Edith's thick blonde hair while she patted his knee and made little soothing noises just as one would to a baby who is upset for some obscure reason.

Hansel blubbered on, "She's saintly!" He cried, not even caring that he sounded ridiculous. "She's a miracle. There never was so sweet a woman! Nor so understanding! I love her, I love her!"

Little Jack and the others in the room exchanged smirkingly understanding glances. Only Frank looked away, embarrassed at the spectacle. Hansel looked up in time to catch the glances. "Yeah," he sneered, "yea-a-ah, you dirty-minded bums!" He sounded more like a child than ever. "You think I want to sleep with my mother, don't you? You would!"

Lula was horrified at the disintegration of the huge man. His size, his age, his whole imposing structure had been reduced to the blubbering of a fat, ungainly infant.

"Well, I don't," Hansel was sputtering, "for your information, I don't. I love her. Is that so unnatural? Is it so unnatural for a man to love his mother. Oh, you rat," he looked up at Jack again. "I know why you brought this up. I know it was aimed at me. So help me, some day I'll kill you!" And he buried his face in Edith's hair again. Edith, although she was caressing his knee, was looking at the others with a half-smile that made Lula shudder.

Little Jack was laughing out loud now. "Boy," he said, "you certainly take the bait. Come on, Hansel, admit you'd like to murder your mother. No, better than that, admit that you would like to take the whip to her. That you would like to draw blood. Come on, Hansel, admit it!"

Lula thought that Hansel would kill the slight, aging comedian. He jerked his head up, almost ruining the carefully planned golden coiffure on Edith's head. He jumped to his feet, pushing the girl out of his way, and almost flung himself across the room until he was standing directly above Jack, who had not moved. It came to Lula that this was a common occurrence, that every time Jack and Hansel got drunk in each other's company, this scene repeated itself. Hansel was breathing heavily. "You slimy piece of dirt," he croaked in his infantile whine, "you rotten, twisted little bully. What are you putting in my mouth? What do you know about my mother? What do you know about me?" He lurched drunkenly for a moment, then he turned away and went to the bar to fix himself another drink with trembling fingers. "She's a saint, I tell you, she's a saint!" He was weeping openly, smashing his grimy fist into his eyes, rubbing and smearing the tears all over his face.

Frank had had enough. He stood up and started toward Hansel to help him. To stop him from making a further spectacle of himself. But Hansel turned on him, spilling half the contents of his new drink as he swung around. "Don't you come near me," he cried. "Stay away from me. Stay away from me or I will kill you!"

Edith apparently thought the time had come to put a stop to it, too. She rose and started toward Hansel. Only Margot and Pee Wee and Jack sat still, watching the scene with relish. Lula was petrified. She was glued to her chair.

Suddenly the huge agent laughed and it was as if he had taken a hold at the top of an exquisite window drape and torn it right down the middle with a ripping, hissing sound. He laughed out loud. And he lurched back against the fireplace. Groping wildly around behind him, he picked up a marvelously wrought cast-iron poker. He brandished it before him.

"Look," he snarled. "Look at this. Come any closer and I'll let you have it right across the head. Stay away from me!" Frank and Edith stopped their advance and he turned away from them as if he had suddenly lost all interest in their presence. He stared into the flames.

"Mother," he muttered. "Mother!"

He knelt down abruptly on the floor, his head hanging almost into the fire, the poker resting listlessly in his right hand. "Mother," he continued. Then he lifted his head, almost falling forward with the effort. "I'll kill you," he muttered. He crouched again, hiding his head in his hands and he looked like a huge medicine man, prostrating himself before the flickering voodoo fire, muttering his incoherent curses under his breath. "I'll kill you," he went on, almost in a whisper. "I'll kill you. Oh, you bitch, you faithless, callous bitch!"

Suddenly he turned on the others and spoke as calmly as if nothing had taken place before. "You know what happened to me?" he asked, just as if he were talking to the gang over a marble game. "I came home one afternoon and found my parents together and do you know what they were doing?" He broke off and turned away again. "You bitch," he muttered, "you bitch!"

Jack broke the spell in a horrible way by laughing out loud. "How do you suppose you came into the world?" he asked jeeringly, and his answer consisted of the loud heartbroken sobs from the enormous man on the floor before the fire.

Now Edith had reached Hansel and he permitted his head to be cradled in her lap and lay there quietly sobbing, sniffling like the aftermath of a baby's crying. He was spent.

Lula watched in horrified fascination as Edith soothed the great, blubbering blob of flesh. She ran her hand through his thinning hair, she pulled his face close against her breasts. Finally she reached out toward Jack, and he, obviously knowing what was needed, handed her her drink.

She held it against Hansel's lips and murmured, "Here, darling, have some of Mummy's drink." Lula almost threw up as she saw both his pudgy hands grasping eagerly around the frosty glass, and his big, loose lips slobbering over the edge of it. She shuddered as she heard the gulping, sobbing sound as he swallowed a good half of the contents. Edith smiled at him and patted him, and it came to Lula that she had been through this same scene before.

Jack was obviously enjoying himself. He had the triumphant smile of an eighth-grade bully and he was preening himself under the eyes of Pee Wee who was looking up at him adoringly in the manner of an adolescent girl with the local football hero.

"Look," Frank said, and he was looking at Margot, "this is a hell of a way to have a party."

Margot was nodding and smiling and suddenly Lula felt the hot eyes on her. She wished then that she were safely back in her own apartment, for there were forces loose in this room that she had never been confronted with before. Forces she did not understand and therefore had no way of coping with.

Margot said, "Sure, Frank, it's a hell of a party this way. Let's do a little dancing." She stood up and between her and Jack passed a look of understanding as he stood up, too, dragging Pee Wee to her feet.

Jack said, "Somebody's got to dance with Edith. Her little boy isn't capable yet. I consider myself elected." He went to Edith and pulled her up from the floor. Hansel's head hit the hearth with a resounding thud, but no one seemed to pay the slightest attention to it and Hansel stayed where he was. Jack and Edith went to the record player and put a dance recording on. They swung out onto the floor, their bodies glued together. Frank looked for a long moment at Lula, then his eyes flitted between Lula and Margot and Pee Wee. Apparently he saw something which served as his cue and he went to Pee Wee, who drifted into his arms and they glided off.

Margot came over to stand before Lula. "Seems that we two women are left to take care of each other," she smiled. She pulled Lula to her feet and put her arms around her and they danced out into the middle of the room. Her thighs were demanding as they touched Lula's.

Lula pulled away. It was an almost unconscious gesture.

Margot stopped dancing and looked down at her. "What's the matter?" she asked.

"I don't know. I'm sorry. I didn't mean to seem rude."

"You weren't rude. You just seemed kind of scared. What have I done to scare you?"

"Nothing," said Lula, "nothing. Please, let's sit and talk."

Margot followed her to her seat while the others kept on dancing. They did not seem to have noticed the brief exchange between the two girls. Lula sat down in her chair. It was as if her knees buckled under her. There was a kind of relief, a kind of refuge, in sitting down.

She looked down at her feet, listening to the others dance and she was painfully aware of Margot sitting across the narrow space from her, watching her, looking at her, staring at her. She shivered a little ...

Hansel was beginning to stir in front of the fire and gradually Margot's attention was turned toward him. He had raised himself to a sitting position and she, as hostess, got up to fix him another drink and give it to him. He gulped it down and she made him another.

Lula herself had two drinks in succession and they helped a lot. She was not reeling drunk, but the alcohol released her to a certain extent, and for the first time, she smiled at Margot, and suddenly Frank was standing over her, looking at her with burning, expectant eyes. She looked around at the crowd that seemed to be hovering over her and smiled. They all laughed and it was as if something had been unlocked. As if some hidden spring had been turned loose.

She listened to Frank exultantly holding forth. "The eyes," he was saying, "the eyes are the most valuable objects that people have been endowed with."

Little Jack disagreed. "The hands," he said, "it's the hands." He held up his hands and turned them before his eyes. "Look at those two miracles!" He flexed his thumb. "See how that little thing fits into the palm? Where would we be without that clever trick?"

Frank shrugged. "Perhaps we'd be better able to keep out of trouble." He plumped into a chair and took a long swallow from his drink. Over the rim of the glass, he was watching Lula intently and she was painfully aware of his eyes. She fidgeted nervously and tried to avoid the scrutiny. Frank continued. "I'm an observer," he remarked, "I am a spectator. As such, I do not become involved. It's a professional disease."

The little blonde Edith spoke up. "You don't mean a spectator," she smiled disarmingly. "You mean a snooper."

Frank did not become angry. He looked at the girl sadly. "I have been called that," he said unhesitatingly. "I have been called a lot of things."

The girl, seeing that she could not pick a fight, became con-trite. "I was only kidding, Frank."

"No," he answered, "you were not, but what the deuce, one name more or less doesn't make a lot of difference."

"Aw, Frank," she said, really disturbed now, "you're an important man. You can make or break people."

"Is that being important? Who is it I can make or break? A bunch of montebanks! In Shakespeare's time they were classed with the rogues and vagabonds and thieves. A lot of them still belong in that category. There's no pride to be found in having that bunch under my thumb."

"But what about all the important people you write about in the night clubs?"

"Important? Is a drunk in a booze joint important?"

"But when you write an exposé. When you reveal their secret vices. Then you're doing a real service."

Frank stood up impatiently. "We've all got secret vices, girl. There's nothing heroic about revealing someone else's vice. As a matter of fact, it smacks uncomfortably of tattling. I don't know why I haven't ended up in jail for libel a long time ago."

Little Jack looked searchingly at Frank. "I thought you liked your work, boy," he said.

"Like it?" Frank went to renew his drink. "I loathe it. But it's like a trap. Once you're in it, you can't get out. If you're at all successful, you become too important to your editor. Or rather, your sources become too important. You can't let go and get into something decent. If you did, someone else would have to start from scratch again, and building up the column would take a long time. Editors don't have that time to spare."

Margot said smilingly, "Indispensable, aren't you, Frank?"

Frank looked at her and a shadow of disgust passed swiftly over his face. "Yeah," he drawled, "I'm about as indispensable as a pile of fertilizer in the middle of the living room."

"Ugh," cried Edith, "you're being vulgar."

"I meant to be," he said drily. The others went back to dancing and Frank sat down by Lula. "You haven't got much to say," he stated.

"I'm better at listening," she smiled. Then she continued, "Why are you so unhappy? You have a wonderful job and a beautiful wife."

Frank looked at Margot where she was dancing, glued to Little Jack. Pee Wee was fixing herself another drink. "I've got a beautiful wife, all right," he said. "Accomplished, too." He sat in silence for a little while, then spoke again. "Too accomplished." He turned suddenly. "Have you ever been to India?"

She shook her head.

"Then you've never seen a flute-playing, swaying, entrancing snake-charmer. Margot has missed her calling. I'm her little hissing, flat-headed cobra. Oh yes, she's beautiful and accomplished."

Impulsively she put a hand on his arm. "You're so bitter," she said.

He sat there staring at the hand on his arm. He touched it lightly with his fingers. But just as he was about to say something, Margot came toward them, her eyes shining unnaturally, her lips moist from her drink.

"Listen," she cried, "Little Jack just had a wonderful idea. Let's play Fumbling!"

Frank looked at her uncomprehendingly. "Fumbling?"

"Yes, you know, that new game. It was written up in *Life* magazine."

He drew a long breath. "Oh," he said. "Oh, yes." He looked at Lula then, and shook his head. "No," he said quickly, "let's not."

"Ah, what's the matter with you? You men go into the bedrooms and find some clothes to disguise yourselves with. When you get through, go out in the kitchen and then we girls will do the same."

They all knew about the game. Everyone would disguise his or her identity with strange clothes and stuffing in appropriate places. Then all lights would be turned out and all would scramble together in the middle of the floor. The trick was to guess someone's identity through "fumbling" in the dark. A cute little game. A calculated little game.

"No," Frank said again. "No, I'm taking Miss Lang home."

His statement was followed by dead silence. Finally Margot said, "Home?"

"Yeah," said Frank, "that's what I said. Home."

Little Jack broke in. "But the party's just begun!"

"I know it's just begun. And this is no place for her." He stood up. Lula sat on the couch, dreadfully embarrassed. She was staring up at Frank with wide open eyes. There was something about him at that moment that appealed to her immensely.

Margot moved closer to Frank. "Do you know what you are doing?"

"I know."

"But … but … you can't."

"I've changed my mind."

Margot turned to Lula. "Do you want to go home?"

"I … I have to go to work in the morning."

"Work?" Margot almost screamed. "Look, honey, we're all in the same business. Work doesn't start until noon."

"I'm working up a new routine."

"Oh, for Pete's sake!"

Frank turned to Lula. "Come on, Lula, let's go."

Lula did not want to go, but she felt instinctively that Frank knew better. She stood up.

Margot leaped at Frank. "Wait," she cried. "Wait! You're just robbing yourself!"

"Remember what I told you, Margot," he said quietly, "not with her."

"What's the matter with you?" She looked around at the others. They were staring, smirking. "Virtuous Frank," she sneered.

"Are you in love?" she asked nastily. "Are you in love with this little tart?"

It went through Lula like a stab and she realized more fully now what company she was in. Well, I asked for it, she thought bitterly. She moved toward the door.

Margot followed her. "If you let him into your apartment," she spat between her teeth, "you'll live to rue the day."

In the cab Lula leaned back and breathed deeply as Frank sat nervously at her side. "Please don't take me all the way," she said.

"I'm taking you home," he answered laconically.

And he did. The cab stopped by her apartment hotel and he got out and helped her descend. He paid the driver and they went together to her door.

"No," she said, "not inside."

But he did go inside and she fixed him a drink and they sat and stared out of the window at the Manhattan skyline and said nothing to each other for a long time.

Finally he said quietly, "Thank you, Lula."

She looked at him in surprise. "What do you mean, thank you?"

"You saved me from doing something tonight I would have been sorry for as long as I live."

"I? I saved you?"

"Yes, you."

"But ... but how? And ... and why?"

"That's a long story, Lula ... it's a long and complicated story. I don't know whether I could tell you or not."

"I know," she said. "Secret vices."

"That's only part of it. Though it's a large part of it. Do you know that I was about to throw you to the wolves tonight?"

"You mean … you mean that game? Fumbling?"

"Oh, no. No, that had nothing to do with it. I never even thought of that."

Surprisingly, he started to cry. She made a small movement of compassion toward him and suddenly nothing made any sense. He sobbed like a child. All of the pent-up stream of remorse, of conscience, of fear, of frustration poured out of him as if through an opened sluice. He sank to the floor, a picture of abject misery.

"Frank!"

She knelt by him and stroked him and petted him as if he were a child. And suddenly she thought of Hansel. Of big, fat, child-like, pathetic Hansel. For here was Frank and Frank was a child, too. Frank, who held Broadway under his thumb. Frank, who cried like a lost child in the dark.

He mumbled something into his balled fists. "Why didn't I meet you before?"

"Before what, Frank?"

He sat up and he looked like an infant, with the baby tears streaming down cheeks. "I'm filth, Lula!" he cried. "Filth!"

She reached her hands toward him where he was crouching on the floor. "Oh, no! No, Frank! No, you're not. You're the gentlest man I know."

"Gentle!" he sneered. Then he dragged himself to his feet and found his drink where he had left it on the coffee table. He took a deep gulp and looked at her almost curiously. "What are you doing with me, girl? What do you want?"

"Want?"

"Yeah. I can do you a lot of good."

She turned away from him. "You'd better go," she said and her voice cried with disillusionment.

"No," he said anxiously, "no, I didn't mean that. You didn't start this. It's a habit. It's just a habit. I'm like a rich girl. I think everybody loves me for my money."

"I don't love you. I … I feel sorry … so sorry for you."

Frank sat on the couch, his body bent over in the classic attitude of grief. "Sorry," he muttered. "You feel sorry for me." Then he cried out, "It's not love, it's pity. Pity!" He sprang to his feet and stood hovering over her. "I hate you!" he cried, "hate you!"

He started toward the door, but Lula did not let him reach it. She ran after him and caught him by the arm. "What's the matter with you?" she said softly as he stopped and looked down into her face.

His eyes were filled with tragedy. His mouth was drawn down at the corners. Lula remembered a picture she had seen in a theatre history book. It had been an illustration of a Greek tragic mask. It had been almost grotesque in its grief. So was the face of Frank. Grotesque in its misery.

"I didn't mean that," he said softly. "I didn't mean what I said."

"I know," she said. "Come here and sit down. You poor boy. You poor, lost, bewildered boy."

Lula felt herself on the verge of a terrific discovery. She was projecting herself! She was opening her heart, her mind, and she was seeing beyond herself to other worlds. Other worlds embodied in the people around her. Frank, specifically. She recognized with sudden impact that she was forgetting her own misery, her own guilt in this guilt-ridden world, in order to lift onto her own shoulders the tragedy of another. Out of her new understanding, she asked a strange question. "Why do you want to kill yourself, Frank?"

The columnist stared at her. "Kill myself?" he repeated as if it were the first time the concept had ever entered his mind.

"Yes, why do you wish to destroy yourself?"

The question was an obvious irritant to him. It made him restless. Insecure. It made him wander across the floor, pick up his drink, go to the window, turn away and return to the couch, where he stood like a small child, twisting the bottom of his jacket. "*Do* I wish to destroy myself?"

"Yes, Frank. Every day, in your thoughts, in your dreams, in your actions, you destroy yourself. What do you do in your column?"

"Lula, my column has nothing to do with this."

"Oh yes it does, Frank. Why do you spend your life, your career, your energy writing it?"

"Oh, what the hell," he turned away impatiently, "to expose the follies of mankind, if you want a fancy phrase."

"You were not exposing the follies of mankind when you wrote that column about me."

"But don't you see? You were beautiful. Exquisite, exciting! You were no folly."

"All right. What about the rest of your columns? Bitter, cutting, sardonic. Tearing the veil from ugly, undercover, shady lives. What about them?"

"Well, what about them? They're my livelihood. I'm the garbage collector of the Great White Way."

"No, you're not, Frank." Lula exulted in her newfound strength. She gloried in her maturity and the growth of her understanding. She saw so clearly. So clearly for the first time in her life. "No, you're not, Frank," she repeated. "You're punishing yourself. When you destroy the playboys, you destroy yourself. You kill yourself. When a man, as a result of your column, leaps to his death from a Park Avenue penthouse, *you* are the one who leaps. When a woman drinks poison in her bathroom because of one of your exposés, *you* are draining the cup. When a man goes to jail because of your revelations, *you* are the one behind bars. Why? Why?"

Frank stared at her. He sat down in a low chair and a great sigh racked his frame. "All right," he said in resignation, "suppose I do want to destroy myself. So do a million other guys in this lost, rotten, insecure world." He smiled bitterly. "Oh, for the granite-hewn patriarchy of the nineteenth century."

She said quietly, "Would that have laved your guilty mind, Frank?"

He sat for a long time, then he said, "No. No, of course, it wouldn't. Only I can help that. No father ... no all-father can ever save me from myself. I must save myself."

She nodded. "That's right, Frank."

"You don't know," he said desperately, "you don't know."

Lula stretched her young body. Her loins ached with her womanhood and with the past remembrances of her womanhood. "I know," she whispered.

"But listen, Lula, listen," he went on urgently. "I'm only half a man. I am a watcher ... an observer ..."

"I remember your saying that at the party."

"Yes, that's what I am. I'm a peeker. I'm a leprechaun in the woods. I'm a Peeping Tom." He looked up suddenly. "I was going to throw you to Margot tonight so that I might watch."

"I know you were. I know it now. I did not know that then, though."

"But don't you see what that means to a man. It's the negation of his manhood. He is reducing himself to the third party."

"Why, Frank? Why?"

"I don't know." He buried his head in his hands. "Oh, these psychoanalytical fellows would have a pat explanation for it, no doubt. No doubt about that. But I don't know what it is." He looked up and smiled twistedly. "That's *my* secret vice."

Lula rose from the couch and went to sit on the carpet by his feet. She put her head on his knees, hiding her face from his view. "Shall I tell you, Frank? Shall I tell you why you are this way?"

"Tell me."

"No," she said, "tell me about your mother first."

He was silent for a long time. He fumbled on the table beside him and found a cigarette. He lit it and inhaled deeply.

"I come from the south," he began, "from a little southern town. My mother was of German extraction. She was a strong woman."

"I know," she said.

"How?" he demanded.

"I know *you*."

"Yes," he breathed, "yes, I see what you mean now. You don't have to tell me. You have told me. She was a strong woman. Women *are* strength, are they not? Where we men are weak, where we flounder around doing wrong after wrong, sinning in our small ways, woman does not sin at all. She knows the correct road. She alone knows herself to be right. She reduces the man to the little boy, the better to control him, the better to mold him to her ideas. She alone can show him heaven or send him to hell. He depends upon her."

"So you would rather watch two women, who know what they are doing and are allowing you to live, than you would risk your own manhood, wouldn't you, Frank?"

"Yes." His assent was like a suppressed explosion. "Yes. You strange and wonderful woman, yes!"

"And you hate yourself for it, don't you, Frank? You have nothing but loathing and contempt for yourself for it, don't you?"

"I hate myself."

"And it's a secret, isn't it? You hide it and bury it and push tons of dirt over the secret, but it's there. It's there all the time."

"Yes."

"Do you see, Frank? When you destroy other people with secrets, you destroy yourself."

He took a deep breath. "Yes, I see."

She moved away from him again. "Would you be afraid to risk your manhood with me?" she asked almost casually.

He stared at her and finally he bent forward and put his head in his hands. "No ..."

"Why not, Frank?"

"Because I love you," he mumbled between his fingers.

"Don't you love Margot?"

He stayed in the same position. "It's strange you should ask me that," he said, "Margot was talking about the same thing at dinner tonight." He hesitated for a while, then smiled crookedly. "The declaration of defeat," he said at last. "No, I don't love Margot. I did, but I don't. There is only one thing she can do for me now." He looked up. "No, that's not true. What I mean is there is only one thing she *could* do. She has done it for the last time and I have watched for the last time. I cannot stand this business of being sick of myself any longer. I'm going to leave her, Lula."

"Don't leave her on account of me, Frank," she warned. "I don't love you."

"I know that," he said. "I am not leaving her because of you, but because of myself. It's just that you have made me see things clearly."

"I'm not so sure it makes me happy to be instrumental in breaking up a marriage."

"It's been breaking up for years." He stood up and stretched. "I'm beginning to feel cleaner already." He laughed and took her hand. "Thank you, Lula," he said. "The first time I saw you during that awesome first strip of yours, I knew that something wonderful would come of that moment. It has. Thank you."

There was a ring at the doorbell. Lula went to the door to open it. Luke strode into the room angrily.

"What's going on here?"

"Nothing, Luke. We're talking."

Luke swore. "Talking!" he snorted.

Lula got angry. Angrier than she could ever remember having been. A good thing had taken place. A happy thing. A great decision had been reached and a life was going to be better for it. She whirled on Luke.

"Get out of here," she shouted. "Get out! Who do you think you are? Are you my owner or something? Do you think you have the right to shove yourself into my apartment like this and spy on what I am doing? Are you my judge? Get out right now!"

He stopped dead in his tracks, looking at the furious girl. "I love you, Lula," he said. He turned on his heel and strode out.

"Everybody loves me tonight," she said. "But everybody!"

Frank smiled. "I'd better go, Lula," he said. "And thanks again. I'm sorry if I've done anything to come between you and Luke."

"It's not your fault, Frank. If he can't trust me any more than that, I doubt very much if he loves me. There can't be much love if there isn't any faith."

"Don't be too hard on him. You see, I understand how he feels. Because I—"

"No, Frank," she interrupted, "we've been all through that before. "Don't ..."

"All right." His smile was one of resignation as he went out the door slowly. "Good night ... and thanks ..."

For a long time Lula stood and stared moodily out the window. She was glad that she had been able to help Frank. But Luke—her fists clenched angrily—that was another story. And not a very pretty one, either ...

When Frank got home the party had broken up. It had apparently been quite an affair. Margot was sitting in an easy chair before the fire. Her clothes were strewn all over the floor. She was reeling drunk, wearing only tiny sheer black panties. No brassiere. Nothing else. She was beautiful ...

His knees shook as he stood just inside the door, looking at her marvelous white body, her full, almost violently pointed breasts that rose and fell with her irregular, drunken breathing.

For a moment he was tempted to hurl himself at her and forget his intentions.

Just for a moment, however. Then he walked past her and into his bedroom. Her glassy eyes followed his every movement.

He pulled a couple of suitcases down from the shelf in his closet and began bundling his clothes into them. He was not aware of Margot's presence until she spoke hoarsely from the doorway.

"You moving in with the little innocent blonde?"

He did not bother to answer her, but continued with his packing. She took a lurching step forward. "I'm speaking to you."

"I heard you."

"Then answer me, damn you! You moving in with her?"

"No."

"Then where d'you think you're going?"

He turned and spoke calmly. "I'm leaving you, Margot."

She laughed drunkenly. "That's what *you* think!"

"I don't think. I'm doing it." He returned to the suitcases, making frequent trips to his dresser and to the closet.

She watched him for a long time. "You won't get far," she muttered. "You'll be back. Only Margot can give you what you like. That little dame hasn't got a thing to hold you with. She hasn't the guts."

"I'm not leaving you for her."

"Then what the hell are you leaving for? Look! Look at me!" She tore the frail panties from her hips and stood naked before him. "You planning to leave all this?"

For the first time since he had known her, Frank looked at his wife's body with disgust. Beautiful as it was, it seemed singularly unattractive at that moment. "Yeah," he said calmly, "I'm leaving all that."

She began to cry. She seemed frightened now and she cried sloppily, dripping great tears on her nude breasts. "Why?" she sobbed. "Why? Haven't I been good to you? Haven't I done every-thing you wanted me to?"

He felt sorry for her and patted her clumsily on the shoulder. "You've been very good to me, Margot. It's just that I can't live with myself any more because of the things we do together. I've got to get away."

"Just for a while?" she asked hopefully. "Just for a vacation?"

"No, Margot, that wouldn't do any good. I'm leaving permanently."

She sank down on the edge of the bed and leaned forward, putting her head in her hands. "But I need you so, Frank. I can't live without you."

Now it was his turn to laugh. "You mean you can't live with-out my column. Don't worry, Margot. I won't do you any harm in my column."

"You'll stop mentioning me."

"No. No, I won't. Don't worry."

"I know you will." She looked up, hate blazing in her eyes. "I know whose name will be in it now."

"Look, Margot, I told you before and I'm telling you again—I am not leaving you because of Lula."

"You love her."

"I wouldn't lie to you. Yes, I love her. But she doesn't want any part of me."

Margot smiled nastily. "What's the matter, Frankie? Couldn't you do it?"

"You *are* a bitch, Margot. No doubt about it." But he couldn't get really angry at her. He wished he could. It would be a lot easier that way.

"Five bucks says you couldn't," she sneered. "I know you. Without a little stimulation you make a pretty poor showing."

He made no answer, but hurried along with his packing. He was almost done and was closing his suitcases when Margot spoke again. She had been watching him intently all the time.

"Don't you love me any more, Frankie?"

"You answered that one yourself at dinnertime," he said drily. Then he picked up the suitcases and started out of the door. He felt better already. It was a good decision. It was going to bring him peace and happiness and fulfillment. He could feel it in his bones.

Margot got up from the bed and followed him, naked as she was, into the living room.

"I'll send somebody up after the rest of my stuff tomorrow," he said as he started toward the front door. There he turned and looked at the white figure, swaying drunkenly in the middle of the firelit room. "Good-by, Margot. And thank you for our years together." He turned and started to leave.

"You're not going anywhere," she hissed at his back. "Put down those suitcases and stop acting like a fool. Put them down, I say."

"No, Margot," he said. "Good-by."

"I'll bust you wide open," she remarked vehemently. "You and the little tart too."

He turned again. "You can't do a thing to me."

"Oh can't I, though. Wait and see. I'll hit you where it hurts the most."

"Margot," he said firmly, "I don't care what you broadcast about me. This has *got* to end."

"You don't care if I lay your little secrets bare in public?"

"Frankly, I don't give a damn. There are other cities, other papers, other jobs, if it comes to that. It would simply make the break cleaner."

"There are other ways of hurting you," she muttered.

"Oh, come off it, Margot," he said and left the apartment.

Margot stood where she was for a long time. Then she went to the bar and fixed herself a stiff drink. She returned to the chair she had been sitting in when Frank had come in. She sat there, naked, for a long time. Then she made a sudden decision, jumped to her feet and dialed a number on the phone.

After many rings a sleepy voice answered.

"Jack?" she asked, "sorry to have gotten you out of bed, but I've got to talk to you. No, it can't wait till tomorrow. Now. I think you'll enjoy what I'm going to ask you to do for me. Come back over here right away. No, leave Pee Wee there."

She hung up the phone and went into her bedroom to put on a robe, humming a gay little tune to herself.

CHAPTER EIGHT

The temper of the cast of principals at the Brunswick Theatre was strange, to say the least, on the following night. Margot was seething, Lula was annoyed, Luke was furious, but strangely, Little Jack Horner was riding the crest of the wave. He was singing in his dressing room and on stage he was positively sparkling. He more than made up for the gloominess of Luke.

(STREET SCENE)

(*Luke enters from stage left. At the center of the stage he is met by Little Jack who seems overjoyed to see him.*)

JACK: Luke! Lukie! Where have you been? Gosh, it's good to see you!

LUKE: Hello, Jack. I've been out of town.

JACK: Out of town?

LUKE: Yeah, looking for girls.

JACK: Looking for girls? You mean you go out of town to look for girls now?

LUKE: That's right.

JACK: But we've got plenty of girls right here. Beautiful girls. Gosh, you should have seen the beauty I had last night.

LUKE: I've had 'em all.

JACK: All the girls in this town?

LUKE: That's right. I've been around.

JACK: Oh now look, that isn't possible. Nobody could have had all the girls in this town.

LUKE: (*Laconically*) I have.

JACK: It's impossible, I tell you.

LUKE: It ain't.

JACK: All right. I'll tell you what I'll do. I'll bet you five dollars that I've had more girls in this town than you have, no matter what you say.

LUKE: That's a bet, you dope. I tell you I've had 'em all.

JACK: That's what *you* say. Tell you what. We'll stand right here and when a girl comes by that I have had, I'll say "Bing!" And when a girl comes by that you have had, you say "Bang!" At the end we'll count up and the one who's had the most gets the dough.

LUKE: Let me get this straight. When a girl comes by that you've had, you'll say "Bing!" And when a girl comes by that I have had, I'll say "Bang!" And whoever gets the most gets the money?

JACK: Right. Oh-oh, hold it, here comes a girl now.

(*A beautiful blonde enters. She sees Jack and rushes right to him.*)

BLONDE: Jack! Jackie! Where've you been keeping yourself?

JACK: Gosh, honey, it's a long time since I've seen you. Where're you living now?

BLONDE: I'm at the Ritz. Say, why don't you come up and see me.

JACK: Sure, sure. I'd love to. How about eight tonight? We'll go out and have dinner. OK?

BLONDE: Sure! I'll be expecting you. (*She flounces past Jack on her way out at stage left.*)

JACK: BING!

LUKE: Hello, honey! (*The blonde stops and looks at Luke.*)

BLONDE: Why, Luke! Why, I haven't seen you for ages.

LUKE: That's right. The last time was … let me see … we went to Atlantic City, didn't we?

BLONDE: Yes, and that night we went out in the sand dunes, remember?

LUKE: (*Reminiscently*) Yeah … yeah, I remember.

BLONDE: (*Laughing*) And somebody stepped on your back.

LUKE: Yeah. And you said, "Thank you!"

BLONDE: Well, why don't you come and visit me? I'm at the Ritz.

LUKE: All right. When did Jack say he was coming up?

BLONDE: Eight o'clock.

LUKE: I'll be there at eight-thirty.

BLONDE: Fine. I'll be seeing you. (*She flounces out.*)

LUKE: BANG!

JACK: OK. We're even. (*They shake hands.*)

(*The Gorgeous Redhead prances in. It's Pee Wee, of course.*)

REDHEAD: Why, Jack! My, I'm glad to see you!

JACK: Hello! It sure has been a long time. Where are you living?

REDHEAD: Oh, I'm at the Ritz. Why don't you come up and visit me?

JACK: That I will. That I will. How about tonight at nine o'clock?

REDHEAD: Fine. I'll be expecting you. (*She prances past Jack on her way out at stage left.*)

JACK: BING!

LUKE: Hello, sweetie!

(*The Redhead stops and sees Luke.*)

REDHEAD: Why, Lukie! Long time no see. You're looking grand. Why, I haven't seen you since … since …

LUKE: Since the time we went to Weehawken, remember?

REDHEAD: (*Fondly*) Oh, yes. Weehawken. The ferry.

LUKE: (*Roguishly*) Woowoo!

REDHEAD: My, that *was* a wonderful night. Remember, I got poison ivy.

LUKE: Yeah, that's what *you* called it. (*He scratches himself.*) Itchy. Feels like I've still got five-and-a-half years to go.

REDHEAD: (*Dreamily*) My, my, what a night.

LUKE: Remember? You said, let's put the little Ford in the garage.

REDHEAD: Yeah. Gosh, and I met you on the street the next day.

LUKE: Yeah. And you called across the street, "How's the little Ford?"

REDHEAD: Yeah. And you answered, "Oh, it's still running!" (*They laugh together.*) Say, I'm at the Ritz, why don't you come up and see me tonight?

LUKE: Fine. I will. What time did Jack say he was coming up?

REDHEAD: Nine o'clock.

LUKE: All right. I'll be there at nine-thirty.

REDHEAD: Okey-doke. I'll be waiting for you. (*She prances out.*)

LUKE: BANG!

JACK: All right. We're still even! (*They shake hands. Jack looks off to right.*) Oh, oh, here come my wife and daughter. Now, no cracks about those other women.

(*Jack's stocky "wife" and beautiful young daughter come in.*)

WIFE: (*While Daughter is making eyes at Luke*) Well, there you are, standing on the corner talking to bums. (*Luke looks around desperately, trying to find the bums.*) Haven't you got anything better to do? I want some money.

JACK: All right. All right. How much do you want?

WIFE: Fifty dollars.

JACK: (*Screaming*) FIFTY DOLLARS!

WIFE: I need a little pocket money. If you'd come home once in a while I wouldn't need so much money for entertainment.

JACK: Money for entertainment? What the hell are you buying?

WIFE: None of your business. Come on, daughter. (*The two women prance past Jack and Luke and out left.*)

JACK: (*Disgustedly*) Bing!

LUKE: (*Triumphantly*) BANG! BANG!

JACK: Why you …! Oh, all right. You win. Here's your five bucks.

(*A swish enters from stage right. He swishes past Jack and Luke, but turns and flicks his handkerchief in Luke's face, before he leaves the stage at left.*)

LUKE: BANG!

JACK: Holy smoke! Here's another five!

(BLACKOUT)

The sweat was trickling down Lula's sides when she returned to her dressing room after her act, carrying her discarded costume over her arm. She shut the door and poured herself a drink. Last night she had thought for a short while that such surreptitious drinking was a thing of the past. But here she was back at it again.

She sank wearily into a chair and took stock of herself.

How long could she go on like this? There was nothing but misery in it. Last night it had looked as if something worthwhile had been accomplished. Then Luke had come to the apartment and it was suddenly as if something good and fine and beautiful had become ugly. And although Frank had apparently done what he had intended to do, judging by the mien of Margot, there was no satisfaction in it any longer. The plum had turned rotten in her mouth.

She was painfully aware that Margot hated her now. Not only had she disappointed the stripper last night, but obviously somehow or other Margot was blaming her for what had happened between her and Frank. Lula did not feel that the blame lay with her. All the same there was a vague, inexplicable stirring of guilt in her. She had not talked Frank into leaving Margot. He had decided that for himself. And she certainly had not *taken* Frank away from Margot. She was not interested in Frank, except as a friend. She was not to blame for the fact that the columnist loved her. She tried hard to make herself feel blameless. But somehow she couldn't. There was an anxiety in her that she could not put down.

There was a knock at her door and she said, "Come in."

Frank stood there.

She did not move. "Does your wife know you are in the theatre?" she asked.

"No," he said and smiled. "I snuck in to see you."

She turned her back and there was a pathetic weariness in the motion. "Don't come to see me, Frank. I did not break up your home. I have to work with Margot. I don't want her to get any ideas."

"She won't, Lula," he said. "I made it very clear to her last night that you had nothing to do with our break-up."

"Then she *did* think I had something to do with it, didn't she?"

"Yes."

"Well, I am afraid to get mixed up in it, Frank. Please, stay away from me."

He pleaded. "Look Lula, I know you don't love me. That doesn't keep me from loving you, though. Please don't send me away. I am free to see you now if I want to. I need you, can't you understand that? You mean too much to me for me just to give you up."

"All the same, you must, Frank. This is not going to be a triangle. I lost Luke because of you last night."

Frank swore. "Oh, that damned fool. I'll talk to him."

She sprang to her feet. "You'll do nothing of the kind. Oh, leave me alone, can't you? All of you? I'm like a pawn being shoved around from one end of the chessboard to the other. Don't I have anything to say about my own life any more?"

"Please, Lula. Don't talk to me that way. Please, I beg you. Ever since that first time I saw you on this stage, I have worshiped you. Please don't tramp on the way I feel about you."

"I'm sorry, Frank. Honestly, I can never tell you how sorry I am, but now all I want is to be left alone. Everything I touch turns rotten in my hands. It's too much! Too much!"

She sank down in her chair again and wept bitterly and he came to stand over her.

"Listen Lula," he said eagerly. "Listen! I know what you want. You want to act, right?"

She shook her head slowly. "I don't know *what* I want any more."

"But *I* know. You want to act. And you're in love with Luke, right?"

She looked up, her eyes blazing. "No! No, I'm not in love with anybody. I just want to be left alone. Leave me alone. Leave me in peace!"

"Lula, Lula! I'll get you into television. You and Luke both. You can get married. You can get on with what you both want to do. Let me help you, please. There isn't a TV producer I don't know. I can set you up and you can forget all this."

"No, no, no! Can't you understand that I said *No? I* want peace, do you understand? Last night when we talked at the apartment, I thought that something good had happened, but today I have found out that there was nothing good about it. Everybody hates me now. Everybody looks at me with loathing. I want some rest. I want to be by myself and do my work and stay out of other people's lives so that they will stay out of mine. I want nothing from you. Please go away!"

Frank looked at her for a long time, then he turned on his heel and walked slowly and sadly out of the room.

For a while there was silence, broken only by the faint sounds of music and laughter from the theatre. Then the door opened slowly and quietly. Lula did not hear it. She sat at her dressing-table, her head cradled in her arms. She would not have heard the atomic bomb go off.

Hansel Schnitzler came into the room. He stood silently at the door, then he moved forward hesitantly, closing the door softly behind him. He went straight to Lula and knelt at her feet. Not until he put his head in her lap, did she realize that he was there.

She raised her face with a startled movement. Then she saw who it was and sat looking down at him. Neither of them said anything for a long time. Finally she stirred under the weight of his head.

"What do you want?"

"You," he said.

She turned her head. "Go away, Hansel," she whispered.

He did not move. His muffled voice came from her lap. "I heard you and Frank. I heard everything you said. You need me, Lula."

"I don't need anybody any more."

"You need me."

"No."

"Yes, you do. Somebody has got to give you protection."

She laughed now. "Who? You?"

He looked up and she was startled to see that his face was puckered like a child's. "Don't laugh at me," he begged. "Everybody laughs at me. Fat Hansel! Mama's boy! Please give me a chance to prove myself."

"Why me?" she asked. "Why not your little Edith or any number of other girls you know or represent. Why me?"

"Because I love you," he blubbered.

Lula was sick of the phrase. It seemed that within the last twenty-four hours everybody in New York and New Jersey had declared his love for her. She was beginning to think that the phrase meant nothing, since it invariably brought misery on the recipient, or else the whole world had gone mad. Or perhaps she had some fearsome quality about her, some aphrodisiac transmission that poisoned every man she came in contact with. She shuddered.

"Don't say that," she begged, but he went on.

"Yes," he cried, his voice muted and muffled in her lap again, "I *will* say it. From the first time I laid eyes on you, I have wanted to be more than your agent."

"Please, Hansel. Forget it."

"I can't forget it. You saw me last night. You know what's the matter with me." He looked up eagerly. "Oh, if you only knew how much you are like my mother. You are so calm, so strong, so … so safe. You're so remote. Please, please don't turn me away. I'll give you everything. Furs, jewels, beautiful apartments, a career unequaled by any other girl in show business. Your own shows, quoting your own salaries and lengths of run. Anything. I will give you anything! But please don't turn me away. I watched you last night. Oh, how I watched you. When you went away with Frank, I nearly died. I drank and cried and drank and blubbered and made a ghastly spectacle of myself like I almost always do, except that this time it was worse. Edith had to put me to bed. I could do nothing. Nothing. She hates me now. She … she laughs at me. They *all* laugh at me."

He was blubbering and sniffling and it was sickening to watch. But through Lula's head went a calculation. She was not by nature, she knew, a calculating woman, but through her head now it ran like a bubbling stream. She was learning. Lula was learning fast. Like the man said in *Death of a Salesman,* she would walk out of the jungle rich!

Yes, she could, couldn't she? If she got nothing else out of the jungle, she *could* get that. Money. Furs. Jewels. A name. A name in lights. Fame. They could all be hers and they were better than nothing. Hansel could do a lot for her. Everyone else turned a cold back to her or else tried to mess up her life beyond recall. She could laugh at them all. *She* could turn her back on *them*. She could make a better life for herself than any of the ones who tormented her enjoyed. And it would take such little effort. Hansel would do it all. And in return … in return … she stopped there. She dared think no further. What would Hansel want from her?

She looked at the huge, quivering tub of a man crouching grotesquely at her feet, and shuddered.

So low had she come then. To this depth had she sunk. Here, then, was the end-all and the be-all of Lula Lang! Here were the dreams of the college actress embodied in the reality of quivering lard.

She shook as though an ague had passed through her body. "All right," she whispered. "All right."

He looked up, jubilation written all over the vast expanse of his face. "Do you mean it?"

"I mean it."

He threw his arms around her and she felt enfolded in his mountainous flesh. She was stifled and nauseated and her head was spinning with the emotional excesses of the last last few days.

She patted his fat cheeks. "What is my end of the deal?" she asked in a choking voice.

"Deal? Deal?" He jumped to his feet and almost screamed as if he were in pain. "What do you mean, *deal?*"

"What do you want from me, Hansel?" she asked patiently, her nerves quivering within her.

"My darling, oh, my darling," he whispered suddenly, "I want nothing from you. I won't touch you. Please, please don't spoil it by calling it a deal. I am not buying you. Remember, I am not buying you. You come of your own free will, because you … you … love me, or you don't come at all. I am not buying you."

He sounded almost hysterical and Lula's pity reached out to him. Men were a mess. Every one of them. Guilt-ridden, fearful, shamed little boys, who begged and pleaded and cajoled and played games. Who fought their pasts, their presents, and their futures. Frightened, haunted, desperate.

She was tired. She had never been so tired in all her life. "All right, Hansel," she said wearily. "It's all up to you."

"Good!" he cried, "good! Then tonight I'll pick you up after your last performance and take you home and when we are home, you can slip out of your things and we can make ourselves comfortable and talk about the future. *Your* future. About the wonderful things we'll do together. And you can stop worrying about anything, because Hansel is going to take care of you. He's going to take care of everything and nothing can touch you any more."

"What do you mean, slip out of my things?"

"Oh, I won't touch you, honey," he whispered, "I won't touch you. Hansel just wants to look. He wants to look at the goodies. Hansel just likes to rub his nose against the window. He has much too much respect for his Lula to touch her. You rest easy, girlie. Hansel is a gentleman."

He waved his hand airily and swung out of the room. He was whistling a gay tune as he went down the hall.

She turned and looked at herself in the mirror again. She shuddered at what she saw reflected there.

"Slut!" She spat the word out bitterly. But then the bitterness slid off her and she felt somehow secure for the first time in months. She had found her haven. It was not the kind of haven she had dreamed about. But it was safe and certain.

Margot was waiting for Frank by the stage door. "Were you looking for me, Frank?" she asked sweetly.

"No, Margot," he said, "I wasn't."

"I know you weren't."

"Then what did you ask for?"

"No reason."

He started toward the door, but she was in his way.

"Let me by," he said.

She asked, "Are you going home?"

"Yes."

"To *our* home?"

"No, Margot. To my hotel."

"You haven't changed your mind?"

"No."

"Is there going to be something in your column about me tomorrow?"

He was getting angry. "If you don't get out of my way, there'll be something all right."

She smiled sweetly. "Are you threatening me?"

"Look, Margot. We went all over that last night. It's all over. We're through. Finished."

"That's what *you* think."

"You can't do a thing to me."

She smiled calmly. "Who said anything about you?" She started to walk off then, but she had managed to put a serious scare into Frank.

He put a hand on her arm. "Margot. Wait!"

She stopped expectantly, saying nothing.

"What are you talking about?" he demanded.

"There are other ways of getting at you, Frank."

"What ways?"

"Sorry. You'll have to wait and see."

He gripped her violently by both arms and held her in a vise. "If anything happens to Lula," he hissed, "I'll know where to look!"

"You're hurting me, Frank."

"Did you hear me?"

"Certainly I heard you. Please let go of my arms."

"If anything happens to her, you'll wish you had never started it."

She tore herself away violently. "Let go of me, I said!" She rubbed her arms. "I didn't start this, Frank. *She* did."

"She had nothing to do with it."

"That's what *you* say."

He was furious with exasperation. "Look, Margot. Knowing you as I do, I can understand very well that you fell in love with her. That you wanted her. I can also understand why you wanted to bring her home. We have done it so many times together. What you were doing looked right in *your* eyes. But you've got to understand my situation, too. I admit that I am in love with her, but I assure you that she will have nothing to do with me that way. I also admit that my love for her has opened my eyes. But that was not her doing. You have got to understand that I look upon our past together as a horror now. It has been all wrong. It has been sick. Put the full blame on me if you must blame someone, but don't drag a perfectly innocent bystander into it. Please, I beg of you."

"Innocent!" She laughed. "Yes, compared to me, she is a lily, isn't she?"

She looked at him for a brief moment and there was something in her eyes besides hatred and vindictiveness. There was sadness and loss and loneliness and a recognition of a life decayed. There was regret. But there was no remorse.

She turned and went to her dressing room. He stared helplessly after her for a short moment. Then, shaking his head sadly, he walked away.

What is lonelier than a theatre after the performance is finished and the audience has gone home? What is more cavernously empty? What is darker and eerier?

An unbelievable metamorphosis takes place. One moment the huge building is a carnival of lights, of laughter and noise, of dancing bodies and vibrating songs. Then it dies. Every night the theatre dies ... to arise from its own ashes like the Phoenix on the following day.

But when the theatre is dead, it echoes with its lifelessness. It is not asleep. It slumbers not. It breathes not. It lies like a dark carcass on the street of glittering lights and men pass it by.

Its coal black maw is permeated with the musty smell of ghosts that seem to whisper in the wings of long-past triumphs and defeats, of glorious men and women who were, but are no more. Of songs that died with their singers. Of Columbines that died with their Harlequins. Of magnificent vistas of great castles and beautiful landscapes, of elegant drawing rooms and gruesome torture chambers, crumbling with the dust and swaying in the drafts under the sky-high grid, rustling softly like the leaves in the forest.

Its echoes hum softly with long-forgotten music and with deathless words that will not stop humming. It murmurs gently with the silvery laughter of elegant women's voices, with the banal inanities of a thousand shabby comedies.

It is its own mausoleum. Its own tomb and its own monument. It is its own morgue, for it contains within itself its own dead body ...

Thus lay the Brunswick theatre at midnight. Dead as death itself. And then two shadows detached themselves from the black velour drapes at stage left. Like ghostly wraiths they stepped away from the dark and clinging folds. And at once they became creatures of solid flesh, for the leather soles of their shoes thundered on the wooden floor. One had the flat sound of a man's shoes. The other had the sharp thump of high heels.

A man and a woman, then.

They crossed the stage rapidly and hurried through the spacious wings at right and through the stage door reached the darkened alley that ran alongside the theatre. Here they stopped. The man, whose face was hidden in the shadow of his hat brim, raised his head slightly and glanced up at the starry sky.

"A good night," he murmured, "a fine night for fun."

He grabbed the woman next to him and pulled her violently close. For a brief second her excited face flashed in the reflection from the streetlamps at the end of the alley. He crushed her close and he was breathing hard.

"Tonight," he muttered. "Tonight."

The woman clung to him.

Then they pulled apart and he grabbed her by the arm and drew her into a recess in the theatre wall.

There in the deep shadows they waited for their fun.

Lula's last performance that night had been something to behold. Sticking closely to the motif of her innocence versus Margot's sophistication, she had drawn her apparent suffering taut as a bowstring until the men in the audience were groaning. She had enjoyed herself. It seemed like a kind of revenge. On the men and on herself. At the same time she had been frightened. It seemed to her as if every day now she was growing into a sinister Circe to work upon all men's desires. She did not want this. At the same time it fascinated and intrigued her. It held her in a dreadful spell. It was as if she were watching herself changing, just as she had watched screen actors change from Dr. Jekyll to Mr. Hyde, faces gradually contorting into horrible masks of evil. She seemed to be slowly changing, too. Some vile poison was gently and gradually dripping down her throat and inundating her heart, and as it took effect, she changed.

She changed from an idealistic, talented little dreamer to an erotic, calculating, cynical, drunken tart.

Would she ever be able to sleep again? Would she ever be able to look ordinary people in the eye again without defiance? Would she ever sing again from a light heart? Would she ever laugh again from a light heart?

As she swung from side to side on the stage, gradually and painfully divesting herself of her clothes, Hansel's gross countenance swam before her eyes. She was doing this for him. She would be doing this for him in the privacy of her home. This very night she would know the lecherous touch of his swollen fingers. She would know the intimacy of his huge carcass.

She was ill. The lights were spinning before her eyes and the roar of the men in the audience was like the wordless howling of the winds of space.

But she finished her act. She marked down another triumph and then she sat down in her costume and pro ceeded systematically to get drunk. When Hansel came to pick her up after the show, she was lying in the middle of the rug on her dressing room floor, all the lamps blazing, an empty glass still clutched in her hand.

Hansel clucked like a mother hen, and squatting down beside her on the floor, he stroked her golden hair gently and murmured childish endearments. He tried to raise her to a sitting position, but she was as limp as a wet sheet. He fetched water from the sink and dashed it in her face with a heroic gesture. It made no difference. She slept in the pool of water on the carpet. He slapped her face, timidly at first and then as he warmed to his task, with greater fervor, finally rocking her head from side to side with great smacking sounds. She slept right on.

After exhausting every trick he knew, he picked her up with enormous difficulty, for although Hansel was huge, he was small in physical vigor and strength. He staggered to the couch with her drooping form and laid her gently among the pillows. Then he opened her dressing gown wide so that she lay there, breathing raggedly, clothed only in her G-string and net brassiere.

He pulled a chair close to where she was lying and sat down with an elephantine sigh. He pulled out a cigar and bit the end off it. He stuck it in his mouth and lit it. Then he sat there contentedly smoking. And looking …

Once or twice, he laid his stubby hand ever so softly on the silken skin of her thigh. Just for an instant. Just for a fleeting second of warm contact.

The hand he touched her with lay open in his lap. He did not handle his cigar with it. He was careful not to touch the palm against anything.

It was half an hour after midnight when Lula finally woke up. Her first movement was an instinctive covering of herself. Then she turned her head and saw Hansel sitting there imperturbably, smoking, his eyes half closed. A shudder ran through her and she sat up, huddled as if she were cold.

"Go outside, Hansel," she said.

He pleaded. "Please let me stay."

"No."

He went reluctantly, closing the door quietly behind him.

Lula took her time dressing. She was in no hurry. She was sick with all the whiskey she had drunk, and her head was aching unbearably. But she was numb. She was blessedly without thought or feeling. For the moment, at least, she had managed to elude reality.

When she stepped outside her door, dressed in a trim little suit with a fur stole swinging from her shoulders, she was brought back to reality with a crash. For there was Hansel still. Waiting patiently. She had had some vague thought that if she could just get him out of the room, he would go away. He had not gone away. He was there waiting for her.

He took her arm solicitously and together they traversed the darkened corridor with its pale blue safety lights and arrived at the stage door. No one was there. The doorman had gone home long ago. They opened the door themselves and stepped out into the cool night.

As they passed the recess in the wall where the two shadows were waiting, Lula was vaguely aware of their presence. Two lovers.

Two lovers seeking seclusion in the night. She and Hansel went quickly past the spot and emerged into the brightly lighted street.

The two shadows disengaged themselves from the darkness and stood looking after them. They put their arms around each other and stood close together, as if they were comforting each other.

"Tomorrow," said the man. "Tomorrow."

The woman huddled close against him.

When Lula and Hansel reached her apartment, she managed to send him on his way. She was tired. She had a headache. She needed sleep …

The sun shot straight, warm beams through the slats of the Venetian blinds when Lula awoke. She lay for a long time, staring at the ceiling in her bedroom. Then she sat up in bed abruptly. She reached for the phone at her bedside and dialed a number.

Luke's voice was drenched with sleep when he answered. "Yes?"

"Luke?"

He snapped to at once. "Yes, Lula? What's up?"

"Would you buy me lunch today? I want to talk to you about television and I want to talk to you about us."

"Sure, Lula!" He sounded as jubilant as a kid. "When? Where?"

She named a time and a restaurant and laughed when she heard his warbled reply. His voice was singing over the phone and she knew that she was doing the right thing.

She swung her legs out of bed and sat on the edge, rumpling her hair, smiling to herself. Then she stood up and stripped the pajamas from her young body. She felt clean again. She felt whole and right and her former ambitions were streaming through her with renewed vigor. Another week, perhaps two, and she would be through with her job at the Brunswick and on her way in television. They would accept Frank's offer of help, and both she and Luke enjoyed a certain fame as entertainers. They couldn't miss.

She took a quick bath and put on her tiny white panties and brassiere. Then she went rummaging in her huge closet. Finally she found what she wanted. A skirt, an old college sweater, a pair of loafers and some fuzzy white bobby sox. She put it all on and looked at herself in the mirror. College. The good old days were back again. Hansel had never existed. She had never been hurt in Centerville. Joe Pastelli had disappeared. Margot was a ghost. The last four months were wiped out. She was going to hike the rounds again. But this time with Luke and with a powerful backer who could really help her. Everything was going to be all right.

She was singing at the top of her lungs when she went to the phone and called some of her old friends in the Village. They were overjoyed to hear from her. Certainly they would be home this afternoon. What did she think? That they had gotten jobs yet? Oh, Bobby was working out at Idlewild, of course, and Louise was selling stockings at Macy's. But none of them were overburdened with theatrical chores. Sure! Why, certainly she could bring a friend! They'd love to have him.

Say, what gave anyway? Was she quitting her lush feed-trough? Oh, of course they had all been to see her. Well, they hadn't come backstage, for after all, well … perhaps she wouldn't want them. And anyway …

Lula laughed. She was back in the swim again and life looked good to her, as it had once upon a time not so long ago. Most important of all, she would be able to live with herself again. She would still show them in Centerville. They would still be proud of her. When she started to appear on television and in the movies, they would soon forget about that … that visit.

She and Luke ate a huge lunch, topped off with enormous banana splits. No drinks. They were like children. They held hands across the table and sneaked a kiss or two. They laughed and kept reminding each other of the term they had always been so fond of, stopgap. Luke balked a little at letting Frank help them. He did not quite trust the columnist and he was still jealous of him, but finally Lula swung him around.

They squeezed into a phone booth together and called him at the paper. Frank laughed when he heard what they wanted and told them he'd be right over. They returned to their table by the window that looked out on a sun-drenched street and consumed another dish of ice cream while they waited.

When Frank arrived he plunked himself down at their table and looked from one to the other. "What's with you?" he asked and both started talking at once. He raised a desperate hand and Lula took over.

She told him everything that had happened since he left the theatre the night before and how she had awakened that morning and looked herself right in the face. She told him how she and Luke felt about each other. She was honest about the temptation it had been to accept Hansel's offer. She was not ashamed to admit that in her defiance, she had wanted all the things he had offered her. But now that was all over and she had won a kind of battle and all she and Luke wanted was his help to start from scratch.

Luke breathlessly corroborated this. He too was honest. He told Frank about his initial objection to his help and Frank laughed.

"Don't worry, Luke," he said, "I know when I don't have a chance. But please don't blame me for trying. You would have tried yourself." Then he was quiet for a while and finally he stood up. "All right," he said, almost as excitedly as if he himself were looking for a job, "let's see what we can do. You two come along with me."

They went to his office and at the end of an hour, Frank had made four telephone calls and made appointments for the following day with four producers. He decided that it would be a good idea if he went along with the two of them since, as he put it, he could perhaps spade the the ground a little deeper than they. At the end of the hour they decided to celebrate with a drink and removed themselves hilariously to the nearest bar where the men had highballs and Lula had a lemonade.

"No more solid drinking for me," she said, and they approved highly.

Frank went back to work and Lula and Luke went visiting. They stopped close by Washington Square and bought an armload of supplies—crackers, cheeses, canned nuts, and gallons of Chianti. Lula assured Luke that if they brought anything else to drink they would ruin the unaccustomed stomachs of the people they were about to see.

They were given a warm welcome by Lula's friends and it was just like old times again. They talked about acting and about art, about the theatre and about music. They talked about painting and architecture and sculpture and politics and sex and Freud and anthropology.

Luke held his own very well and Lula was in seventh heaven. Gone were the ugly months behind her ...

The time came, eventually, when they had to return to reality, however. Lula's first show was at five in the afternoon, and of course, she could not miss it. Luke and she said good-bye amidst many reassurances that they would all get together again very soon and left in a spirit of high hilarity.

They took a taxi to the theatre together and in front of Lula's dressing room door they exchanged a last kiss. Luke was through at night before Lula was, so they made an arrangement whereby he was to go to her apartment as soon as he finished and start preparing some hamburgers and a little nightcap.

"Then may I stay?" he asked.

"No," she said, "not yet."

He understood and did not press the point. He took her apartment key and went to his own dressing room, whistling a merry tune.

Lula opened her door and stepped inside.

Hansel was waiting for her. "Hello, Lula," he said sweetly, a hidden dagger in his tone.

She looked at him in amazement. Who was this? A ghost from her past. Hansel Schnitzler! Who was Hansel Schnitzler? What did he mean in her life? Nothing any longer. He was part of what she had forgotten.

She smiled, simply because she felt like smiling. She almost laughed out loud, but then she thought he might misunderstand her, so she controlled herself.

"Hello, Hansel," she sang gaily. "You'd better get out of here, I've got to dress."

He did not move. "Where have you been all day?"

"What do you mean, *where?*"

"I called and called. You didn't answer."

"I couldn't. I wasn't there."

"That seems obvious, doesn't it? Where *were* you?"

She looked thoughtfully at him for a moment. "Why?"

"I think I've got a right to know." His voice was taking on an ominous tone.

"Why should you have a right?"

"Perhaps you have forgotten. We made a deal last night."

Now she did laugh. "Oh, Hansel, what *you* said. I thought you didn't want it called a deal."

"No matter what I said, you promised."

She became suddenly serious. "You're right, Hansel. I beg your pardon. I *did* promise and you *do,* because of that, have the right to know where I was when you couldn't get me on the phone."

"That's better," he said in a self-satisfied way. "Well?"

"I was with Luke, Hansel. With Luke and Frank. Luke and I are going into television together."

"You're what?"

"We're leaving burlesque and going into television together."

Now it was Hansel's turn to laugh. An amazed, astonished, explosive laugh. He looked her up and down, dressed as she was in her bobby-sox and sweater. "In that outfit? What are you going to play? Grade school girls?"

She looked down at herself, a little abashed. She had not had time to go home and change her clothes, and anyway she had forgotten about her outfit. She had been so happy and the clothes had gone with her return to sanity.

She laughed a little at herself. "No," she admitted, "that was an impulse this morning."

"I suppose that dumping me was an impulse this morning, too?"

"I am not dumping you, Hansel. It would never have worked out. I am sorry, I just can't go through with it."

He did not move. He sat there like a huge Buddha, his eyes small and mean, his mouth puckering up as if he were going to cry. "And what about me? Have you thought what this is going to do to me?"

She felt dreadfully sorry for him. After all, she *had* made an arrangement with him and then had gone ahead and done something else without even letting him know. She went to him and touched his thinning hair. "I'm sorry, Hansel. I'm awfully sorry. I love Luke."

He looked up quickly. "Since when? Since this morning?"

"Since a long time, Hansel. I have just been mixed up, that's all. What I promised you last night was part of my mix-up. Please release me?"

"And what if I don't?"

"I guess I'll just have to go anyway."

He was crying now. Great tears were running down his fat cheeks. "I'm not going to let you, Lula," he cried. "I can't give you up. You promised me. You promised me!" He beat his fists against his thighs like a little boy in utter frustration.

Lula found herself treating him as if that was what he was, a little boy. She patted his shoulder maternally and murmured, "Come on, Hansel, be a big boy. I've got to dress. You run along now. Come on," she cajoled when his crying only increased and he sat there stubbornly, as if he would never budge. "You'll find another girl. Won't you, Hansel?"

"Never," he blubbered, "never! I'll never find another like my Lula. Please, please don't leave me! I'll be so lonely!"

"All right, all right, Hansel, you stop it now. Come on, get up. Get up!" But she couldn't raise him from the chair.

"I'll do something to myself," he cried, "I'll kill myself. You'll be sorry!"

Even the spectacle he was making of himself could not destroy Lula's good humor. She patted him again on the head and went behind a screen and changed. When she went onstage to perform, he was still there, stubbornly clinging to the chair, crying as if his heart were broken.

Lula's act that night was not the usual one and Margot was seething even worse than she had the night before. Lula felt wonderful. She felt free and light and airy. She flung herself into her performance with an abandon that had nothing of the shy, innocent, frightened, and embarrassed girl in it. As she spun across the stage, she was laughing unashamedly. She was thinking of Luke and she was thinking of what she was going to say to Joe Pastelli after the evening's last show. She was going to free herself from the trap she had fallen into. Yes, she could see the light of day again!

When she returned to her dressing room, Hansel was gone. It made no difference to her, except as a further cause for rejoicing.

She and Luke had supper together, spreading out the hot food from the restaurant across the street on her dressing-table and drinking together from a wine bottle, as if they were children sharing a soda pop. They laughed a lot and they held hands and they shared bites from the same plate and once they clung close together and Luke put his hand over Lula's breast and for *a* short minute the world whirled around them as their breaths came hard and fast against each other's lips. Then Lula extricated herself.

"Not yet," she said. But her smile bore such promise when she said it that Luke took no offense, although he was trembling with his want of her.

And then the evening was over and Lula did not get to see Joe Pastelli, because he was gone at the end of the last show. Luke was gone, too, to her apartment to arrange for their midnight snack and Lula was alone in the theatre. She dressed rapidly, humming to herself. Before she left her room, she picked up the phone and called her apartment and Luke answered. She told him to put on the hamburgers and pour the drinks. She was on her way.

Then she swung out of her door, wearing a bright, light green dress and her fur stole.

When she stepped outside the theatre into the dark alley, it happened. She should have known that it was lying in wait for her. No one had the right to be so happy and so carefree.

The shadow disentangled itself from the dark recess beside the stage door and put an arm around her shoulders. "Where're you going, little girl?" it said in a muffled, trembling voice.

Ice ran through Lula. It had been too good. Too safe. Too carefree. The dreadful lurking thing was about to happen to her. A chill enveloped her like a deadening mantle and she stood there petrified, her knees shaking a little.

"Home," she said.

"To your lover?"

"Let me go."

She became aware of another shadow, deeply entrenched in the darkened doorway. Somehow she was aware that it was a woman. Somehow. She did not know how. She heard the shadow's heavy breathing. She could almost smell the tension and the expectancy in the soft air.

She started to scream, but something soft and muffling was suddenly thrown over her face and through its folds she heard the voice speaking, not *to* her, but *at* her.

"There are those of us who don't approve of what you've been doing."

"What do you mean?" She choked on her words.

"Never mind what we mean. We think it's time for you to learn a little lesson."

She felt a powerful hand at the neck of her dress and then the garment disappeared from her shoulder and back as if an unmerciful hurricane had ripped it off. Her slip followed and then her brassiere.

"Leave her pants on," the woman's voice whispered.

"Why?"

"You heard me. Leave them on."

The first blow hit her then and she heard the woman in the darkened recess groaning with pleasure. "Again!" the woman's voice croaked. "Again!"

The second blow hit her then and drove the breath from her. By some miraculous contortion the man had managed to land the first blow flat-handed across her back, covered only by the skin tight little panties. It stung more than it hurt, but the second blow was dreadful. It sank into the softness of her stomach and doubled her up.

Then the assailant went really to work on her. He covered her body systematically from top to toe. He belabored her breasts until they felt raw and bleeding. He smashed her face until it felt pulpy under his fists. His knee kept slamming into her thighs and groin.

She was on the ground. Still conscious. She could hear the sobbing breathing of the woman spectator and the hoarse, rattling breath of the man. She became vaguely aware of the endearments that were pouring from his mouth as he beat her.

"Little dove," he rasped, "little soft flesh under my fingers! Weep, little girl. Weep and cry out. Please! Please! I want to hear you cry. Oh, I love you. Oh, that soft, soft, suffering flesh!"

She tried to scream. She tried to cover herself, to defend herself, but it was to no avail. She was muffled, gagged, and hamstrung by the wiry hands of the attacker.

Then, on a screeching roller coaster of maddening pain, she plunged into oblivion ...

Everything was white. The air was permeated by a sickeningly penetrating odor that seemed to hang like a smog around her.

Lula opened her eyes and the whiteness blinded her and struck her brain as if a physical kick had been aimed at the top of her head. She twisted her face from side to side, trying to avoid the blinding agony that went with her opened eyes.

A face was bending over her. She closed her eyes quickly, shutting out the disturbing, insistent presence. She waited. It seemed like hours, then she opened her eyes again and the pain struck her a renewed blow.

She was desperately intent on facing whatever it was that was staring at her. She turned her head and forced her eyes into focus.

The face belonged to a nurse.

The face said, "Well, good morning!"

Lula did not know what to make of that. Good morning! What morning? What was good about a morning so riddled with pain?

She tried to smile. It felt as if she were deliberately trying to tear her own face apart with steel tongs. She cried out with the pain and the face said soothingly, "Just lie still, honey. Don't try to do anything."

"Where am I?"

"Hospital."

"But ... but why?"

"Honey," said the voice, commiseratingly, "somebody sure beat you up."

"Beat ... beat me up?"

"Yeah, really belabored you."

"But ... but why?"

"That's what we hope you can tell us. Who was it?"

Lula became aware of other faces. They hovered around her, staring.

"Can you talk, honey?" It was the nurse again.

"It hurts."

"I know it hurts. But these gentlemen are from the police department. They want to know what happened."

"I don't know what happened." Her mind wandered again. "That theatre was so empty. It was so empty. I just went outside the door. They beat me."

"Yes, honey, we know they beat you. Who are *they*?"

"I don't know. A man and ... and ... a woman. The woman only watched."

"But who?"

"I ... I don't know."

She was a knot of pain. An arching, tensed knot of piercing pain. Her breasts felt as if they had been kicked and her loins were a mass of soft, pulpy blood. What in heaven's name had happened to her?

She drifted off again ...

Five days later Lula was sitting up in her hospital bed. She had told the police everything she knew about the assault and they had gone away looking very efficient and very sure of themselves, but she had not heard of anything indicating that they had gotten anywhere in their investigations.

Lula's mind was a screaming vessel of revenge. *She* knew. Even if the police did not, Lula knew who to blame and who to get for what had happened to her.

Margot. This was Margot's doing. She wouldn't have told the police in a million years. This was her affair. This was something another woman had done to her and she would handle it herself. She did not need the police.

Luke came to see her. He was horrified at what had happened to her, but she sent him on his way. This was between her and Margot and Margot was going to pay.

Luke was sick. Here again he was relegated to a backseat. He loved Lula and Lula had assured him that she loved him. But she would not let him help her.

"This is between me and somebody else," she said, and that finished the conversation. He tried to break through her determination, but got nowhere.

Frank came to her and she took one look at him, looming in the door. She cried, "Get out of here! Get away from me. Look what you have brought me."

He tried to remonstrate with her but she would not listen. She was like a tigress. Her mind was seething and her claws were bared. No ordinary male could cope with her.

Frank knew what had happened and he too marked this down as his personal business. It was not the law's. It was his.

He went looking for Margot. But Margot had moved. She was no longer in the old apartment and Frank searched in vain. The more he looked, the more desperate he became.

Frank started drinking. He knocked himself into utter oblivion.

Several times he went to the Brunswick Theatre and watched his wife go through her torrid act. Each time he went there, he went with the intent to punish her for the evil she had wrought, but each time he stood spellbound at the back of a box and watched the lascivious gyrations of the body which he still, strangely, desired to the point of madness. Each time, he staggered from the theatre straight into the arms of alcoholic unconsciousness. Margot's white body was a symbol. It was a symbol of many years of wonderfully exhilarating experiences together. He could not destroy it.

Frank's editor despaired of his columnist during this period. He would grope his way into his office at the paper and stutter out a column on his dictaphone that displayed the utmost contempt for even the most rudimentary human dignity. He did not care. He did not care what he did or said. Most of the time he did not *know* what he was doing or saying or writing.

Finally his editor stopped the column, explaining blandly that Powell was on a vacation. Frank did not even know it. Every day he stammered out an incoherent column filled with mudslinging and invective. Every day his column went into the editor's wastebasket. Frank never read his columns after they had been published, so he did not know that he was no longer represented in his paper.

His editor had decided to sit out this emotional hurricane that was raging through the columnist's private life. Frank was a valuable man. He would be valuable again when he came to his senses.

Frank was drunk almost continuously. Nearly every night, he would stand at the back of a box of the Brunswick and watch his beautiful, evil wife with burning eyes. Every night he would slink away defeated.

His hopeless love for Lula and his hatred of his wife had become a madness with him.

On the third day, when Lula had arrived at something vaguely resembling coherence, Hansel visited her in the hospital. He wept over her and promised her the sky, if she would only let him help her. She was surprisingly amiable. He did not know what to make of it until he understood that her one consuming ambition in life now was to enjoy a complete and full revenge upon the exotic Margot Diego.

He promised her ecstatically that anything that was within his reach and power was hers, if she would only come to him.

She finally accepted his offer. She realized that the best and most thorough way in which she could destroy Margot would be to hit her where it hurt the most, namely through the profession. Hansel promised to quit handling the stripper and to secure for Lula all the spots he would otherwise have placed Margot in.

He was perfectly aware of Lula's reason for giving in to him, but he did not care. He was consumed with love and desire for her. He would have done anything to secure her loyalty.

He left the hospital like a boy who has just pinned his first girl with his high school fraternity pin. He was walking on air. His imagination built his desire for Lula into tremendous, skyscraping heights until he convinced himself that the girl actually loved him. When he arrived at this Mount Olympus, he began seeing himself in the role of defender and his childishly adventurous blood began to boil at the horror visited on his innocent love.

Hansel knew every member of the cast at the Brunswick. He knew at whose door to lay the sadism that had gone into the attack on Lula. He would confront Little Jack Horner with his crime and make him cringe in abject penance. He, Hansel Schnitzler, was for once going to rise to the occasion and prove himself a man.

He put it off until a propitious time would present itself. And as the days went by, his righteous anger mounted until the time came when Lula was released from the hospital.

Hansel went to pick her up and was startled at the tight-lipped, white-faced girl who came down into the lobby from the upper reaches of misery. He suggested that she go to her apartment and return to bed for a good long rest, but Lula responded that she was rested. She wanted to go back to work. There were things to be done that could not be done while she was lying on her back at home.

He drove her to the theatre.

The drive there finally decided him. The time had come. She sat close to him, demurely, her palms lying open in her lap, and her presence fanned the latent knighthood in his boyish heart into whitehot flame. Tonight he would confront Little Jack with his wickedness. The two would have it out and Jack would be hauled away to be hurled into the deepest, dankest dungeon, to languish away the remainder of his mortal days in dreadful expiation of his sins.

Hansel felt good. He felt strong. He felt grown-up for the first time in his life. He felt as if the stranglehold of his mother was being gradually eased from around his throat. After this night he would be free. And Lula would be his.

He pulled his big Cadillac into the alley beside the theatre and the two got out and went inside.

Joe Pastelli met them at the door. He clucked over Lula like a mother hen and patted her shoulder and assured her that he had never heard of so dreadful a thing in all his life. But was he glad to see her back. Why, the show had dropped and dragged its ... its ... well ... heels, since she had been gone. Now they would all pep up and give 'em hell again. It was good to see her. It was great.

He escorted her to her dressing room, rubbing his palms together like a latter-day Uriah Heap. Lula looked along the corridor and into the wings for a glimpse of Margot. But Margot was not to be seen.

She closed her door and proceeded to don her costume ...

CHAPTER NINE

The Brunswick had a full house. Word had spread that Lula Lang was back at work again and men had come from the far reaches to witness her triumphant return. There was a bustling and a crowding in the lobby. Cigarette smoke curled from the doors of the men's room, blending its fragrance with the ever present odor of staleness that always hangs like a pall over burlesque-house restrooms. There was a never-ending stream of unattached males pouring like the flow and wash and ebb of the ocean tides up and down the shabby carpeted aisles, looking for seats in advantageous spots as close to the stage as possible. Men saw each other and recognized each other and either called cheery hellos or tried to hide in the throng so that they might not be hailed. There was a restless stirring and shuffling of feet. In the theatre itself the heavy stench of popcorn was mingled with the sharp smell of impatient, male sweat.

Lula was back!

The audience coughed its way through the pitchman's frenzied "give-away" patter of fancy gifts shrouded by cheap candy, his heavy-handed sales talk of "Genuine Parisian Magazines ... that leave nothing to the imagination." They had not come to listen to him. They glanced impatiently at the heavy velour curtains. They stirred eagerly when the orchestra began to file out from the small door under the stage and into their seats in the pit. That was the signal. The time was coming. They moved restlessly and the pitchman gave up.

"On with the show, Professor!"

Lula was back!

(STREET SCENE)

(*The curtain rises on the downstage area. It is backed by a drop on which is painted a city street lined with little shops. Little Jack Horner enters from one side and Luke enters from the other.*)

JACK: Well, Luke, what are you doing here on the Street of All Nations?

LUKE: Hello, Jack. Well, a friend of mine told me that if I would just come here and stand on this corner, I could get a chance to taste the dishes of all kinds of nations. You know how I like to eat. He told me that this is the street where the girls of all nations cook their national dishes and then sell them in the street to anyone who wants to buy.

JACK: That's right.

LUKE: Oh, boy, I can't wait to taste some foreign dishes.

JACK: (*Looking off stage*) Well, here comes a girl with a dish now.

(*A little Dutch girl in an off-the-shoulder blouse comes out from the wings. She stops by Jack and Luke. They look at her and then at each other and wink broadly.*)

LUKE: (*Suggestively*) Hel-l-l-o-o-o!

GIRL: (*Suggestively*) Hel-l-l-o-o-o!

LUKE: What've you got there? (*The girl is carrying a tray on her shoulder.*)

GIRL: (*Looking at small sandwiches on tray*) Meaty-pie!

LUKE: Meaty-pie? What's that?

JACK: It's a Dutch dish, can't you see that?

LUKE: How am I supposed to know that?

JACK: Look at those wooden shoes she's got on. That means she's Dutch.

LUKE: Oh, I see. Well, Dutchy, give me one of them Dutch dishes. (*The girl gives him one and he chews on it contentedly.*) Um-m-m! It's good. Here's some money for you. (*He gives the girl some money and she prances happily off at the other side of the stage.*) Say, this is good. Have some?

JACK: No, no thank you, I've tasted it before. I come here often.

LUKE: Sa-a-a-y, this is terrific! (*He finishes the sandwich.*) I wish some other girl would come along. This is a fine idea. Do I like to eat!

JACK: (*Looking off stage*) Well, here comes another one.

(*A Chinese girl, carrying a tray on her right shoulder comes on stage. She goes to stand by Luke and Jack.*)

LUKE: (*Suggestively*) Hel-l-l-o-o-o!

GIRL: (*With a thick "Chinese" accent*) Hel-l-l-o-o-o!

LUKE: What've you got there?

GIRL: Pie-e-e-e-eeeh!

LUKE: What?

GIRL: Pie-e-e-e-eeeh!

LUKE: (*Turning to Jack*) What the hell is that?

JACK: Pie, you dope. Pie, like in pie-eyed.

LUKE: Aw, PIE! Well, here, honey, I just had some wonderful pie. Give me some of yours. (*He takes a big piece and bites into it with relish. He chews contentedly for a little while. Then he grows gradually bug-eyed and begins to choke on his mouthful.*) What … what is this? (*The girl shrugs. She does not understand.*) What's in this pie-e-e-e-eeeh? (*The girl does not understand.*) What's the meat in it? (*The girl shrugs. Luke is getting desperate. He keeps chewing with a dogged, insistent motion.*) It tastes like … (*He chokes.*) … I just couldn't tell you. What is it? (*The girl still does not understand him. Luke swallows manfully.*) Is it veal? (*The girl looks uncomprehendingly at him.*) Is it … you know … (*He pantomimes a little calf with horns.*) … Moo! Moo!

GIRL: No. Is not duck.

LUKE: (*Double-take*) Duck? Who said anything about duck? Well then, is it pork? (*The girl looks uncomprehendingly at him with wide eyes.*) I mean is it a little piggy? (*He pantomimes a little piggy at the feed-trough.*) Oinck! Oinck!

GIRL: (*Imperturbably*) No. Is not goosey-pie.

LUKE: Goose? (*He turns to Jack in despair.*) Who said anything about a goose?

JACK: Maybe the girl is daydreaming. You know—wishful thinking.

LUKE: (*Turning to girl*) Well then, what the hell is it I am eating?

GIRL: (*As she is leaving the stage. Over her shoulder*) Me-e-eo-o-w!

(*Luke gags uncontrollably, just as the third girl enters the stage. She is obviously Spanish or Mexican or Latin-American or some such derivative. She is not carrying any tray at all. She stops by the two comedians and glances at them in a way that can not be misunderstood.*)

LUKE: Well, well, well, what have we here?

JACK: That's a Mexican girl.

LUKE: What is she selling?

JACK: *Frijoles.*

LUKE: Free what?

JACK: *Frijoles.*

LUKE: (*Grabbing the girl and starting out at stage left*) Free holes! I'll take a dozen.

JACK: Just a minute. Don't you want to learn about her native customs?

LUKE: That was where I was going. To learn about her native customs.

JACK: No, no, no. Listen to me. Let me get her to tell you about life in Mexico!

LUKE: Do, do! I'm all ears. (*He turns to the audience.*) Free holes! Oh brother, what a country!

JACK: (*To the girl*) Look, my friend here is interested in finding out about your native customs. Tell him something about them.

GIRL: (*Heavy "Spanish" accent*) Well, every moonlit night I sit on my piazza.

LUKE: On her ... WHAT?

JACK: Listen to her and shut up. On her piazza.

LUKE: (*Looking surreptitiously at the girl's back*) Well, it looks comfortable.

GIRL: (*Goes on undisturbed*) And then my lovair comes and stands under my piazza.

LUKE: (*Incredulous*) He comes and stands *under* your piazza?

JACK: Yes, certainly, listen to her, won't you? Quit heckling her.

LUKE: But ... but ... but *under* her piazza. (*He sneaks another surreptitious look.*)

JACK: Certainly. They have very large piazzas in Mexico.

LUKE: (*Staring at the girl's back*) Oh, I don't know. Maybe her lover is a dwarf.

GIRL: (*Rapturously*) Then my lovair takes out his guitar.

LUKE: Ah-ha! I knew we would get to this sooner or later? How big is his guitar?

GIRL: (*Holding her hands way out in front of her*) It is very big. This long. (*Luke is bug-eyed at the size of the guitar.*) And then he strums his guitar.

LUKE: Right in front of you? How long does he strum it?

GIRL: Oh, a very long time. But then he gets tired.

LUKE: I'll bet he does. And then what?

GIRL: Then I strum it for him.

LUKE: Oh, no! No, what a wonderful country! Free holes! And girls strumming your guitar! Oh, what a country. (*He grabs the girl and starts off at stage left.*)

JACK: Hey, wait a minute. Just a minute! Where are you going?

LUKE: I'm going to take this girl out in the moonlight and let her strum my little ukulele!

(BLACKOUT)

Hansel caught Little Jack just as he was coming off stage.

"I want to talk to you."

"OK. Talk."

"No. I want you to come outside with me."

They went out into the alley and ended up standing right in front of the recess where the two assailants had hidden just a few days ago. Hansel confronted the wiry comedian.

His knees were trembling, but he went on manfully. His mind was made up. He was the shining knight on the white charger. "Look, you," he said, "I know what you did to Lula the other night. And believe me, you are not going to get away with it."

Jack smiled. Through his warped mind ran the image of Hansel a couple of weeks ago at Margot's party. He stepped a little closer to the fat man and whispered, "You scare me, fat boy. What are you going to do about it?"

Hansel put his trembling hands up.

This was it, then. This was the moment he had wanted for all these years. When he had been backed into the corner of the schoolyard in his boyhood days, this had been the moment that was building up. This had been the day that everything had been growing toward. He was confronted with the ultimate bully. Here was his chance to justify himself. His chance to make a new start in life. This time it was going to be him and him alone against physical forces, and this time he was going to conquer. He was going to do it himself. He was going to fight a fair fight, man to man, and he was going to win, and after that he would be able to live with himself and confront Lula, not as a blubbering coward, but as a man. As a man in his own right.

He never even felt the blow that slammed him into the pavement and sent him screaming for help.

Lula turned the bottle of Scotch upside down. It was empty. They were always empty when they were needed the most. She looked into the mirror over her dressing-table and saw a contorted mask of hatred. She did not recognize herself at all. It was as if a certain objectivity had entered into her consciousness that made her regard herself from a detached viewpoint.

She knew now that she was going to get Margot. She was going to triumph over the woman who had injected evil into the flowing stream of her life.

She went out to stand in the wings and watch Margot's swan song. She wanted the little pleasure of gloating over her knowledge that this was going to be Margot's last engagement. It didn't matter how good she was. She was fin ished.

She, Lula, would see to it that Margot was finished.

The shot caught her completely off balance.

The policeman who had answered Hansel's desperate scream for help heard the shot, too. But at the moment he was deeply involved in trying to straighten out the mess he found himself in the midst of. He blew his whistle frantically and other policemen came on the run to take care of whatever it was that had happened on the inside of the Brunswick Theatre.

He had charged into the alley upon hearing the squealing calls for help. He had gotten there in time to discover a huge, fat slob groveling on the pavement, a small wiry man standing over him, teeth bared, fists clenched, urging the fat boy to get on his feet and fight. The huge man was slobbering and weeping and sniveling. His cowardice was written all over his face. He crawled toward the shiny shoes and well-creased trousers of the cop, begging for protection and throwing out all sorts of accusations against his conquering opponent.

The policeman booked them both.

The fat man ended up in an asylum, where he sat for two years after that, sucking his thumb, playing with his toes, crying for his mama.

The wiry man ended up in jail for eight years.

The puzzle of the beating of Lula Lang had been solved. The prison mental ward came to know Little Jack Horner very well. He became known as the prisoner who stole pliers from the electric shop in order to tear out his nails so that he might watch his fingers bleed.

The cops who carried out the lifeless body of Margot Diego noticed a small blonde girl in a state of virtual collapse. She was clutched in the arms of a grotesquely costumed comedian.

He was murmuring, "Now, Lula. Now, we can forget it all. We can start again, Lula. They are waiting for us. The producers that Frank called are waiting for us. Please, Lula, don't cry."

The man in the dinner jacket handed over his still smoking gun quietly. Gripped between two burly policemen, he stood silently, his head bowed—watching his wife's life seep away. Frank Powell would never write another column ...

www.ingramcontent.com/pod-product-compliance
Lightning Source LLC
Chambersburg PA
CBHW022047240626
47154CB00007B/2607